Charity Girl

A Nellie Bly Novelette

Copyright © 2020 by David Blixt

Cover by Robert Kauzlaric

ISBN-13: 978-1944540456

www.davidblixt.com

Published by Sordelet Ink
www.sordeletink.com

CHARITY GIRL

A NELLIE BLY NOVELETTE

DAVID BLIXT

EDITED BY ROBERT KAUZLARIC

SORDELET
ink

CHARITY GIRL

CONTENTS

Author's Note

The events of this novelette take place immediately following the novel *What Girls Are Good For*, in which Elizabeth "Pink" Cochrane becomes a reporter, taking the pen-name Nellie Bly. She writes stories focusing upon the poor, the dispossessed, the cheated and swindled. Most especially, her stories focus upon working women.

After three years of writing for the *Pittsburg Dispatch*, she moves to New York City and goes undercover at the insane asylum on Blackwell's Island to expose the mistreatment of the women held there. Her story is published in the pages of Joseph Pulitzer's *New York World*, and makes her a star.

This is what happened next . . .

Dear Sister,

I have an unfortunate girl in my parish who has given birth to an illegitimate child. She is so circumstanced that if it were known it would greatly injure her and at the same time give rise to a great deal of scandal among her friends. She is truly repentant and has brought the child to me to be baptized. (Its name is Louis.)

I therefore request of you the favor to receive the child in the asylum and free her from the burden which she has been so unfortunate to bring upon herself.

Greatly obliged.
Yours respectfully
REV. L. A. Mazziatta
Police Department of the City of New York,
Precinct No. 20

ONE

"I'M GOING TO BE A published author!"

I said this aloud to my empty apartment, so there was no one to hear my exciting news. I had just signed the lease, and had barely a stick of furniture. That didn't trouble me—eager as I was to outfit my new home in New York City, I didn't want to buy anything that was less than perfect. Having pinched pennies since the age of six, I knew better than to play the drunk when flush. *You never know when disaster will strike.*

In fact, disaster had struck almost exactly a month earlier. On the twenty-second of September my bag had been stolen, and it contained nearly one hundred dollars: all the money I had in the world. I couldn't even afford to pay the rent on my shabby little furnished room uptown.

However, the experience made me realize something about myself: crisis brought out the best in me. When pushed to the brink, I could be devilishly resourceful. That night I borrowed enough money to take me downtown to Newspaper Row and marched into the offices of Joseph Pulitzer's *New York World* and pitched them a story.

They didn't buy it.

Yet Pulitzer's prize editor, Colonel Cockerill, was impressed by my pluck and gumption, and he suggested a different story: getting myself incarcerated in the Woman's Lunatic Asylum on Blackwell's Island to expose the goings-on there. At the time, I had no idea it was a repeat of a stunt performed a decade earlier by a man. All I knew was that it was a chance to prove myself—while also peeling back the curtain on misdeeds against women. So I played shatterpated and got myself committed.

I'd emerged three weeks ago—*Was it only three weeks?*—with a story that had made my moniker a household name. Well, not my *actual* moniker. No one knew who Elizabeth Cochrane was. But everyone knew the name Nellie Bly.

Which was how I ended up with the letter in my hand. It was from the publisher Norman L. Munro, offering me more money than I could have hitherto imagined for the rights to publish my story from the madhouse: a whopping five hundred dollars! Considering that I had started off at five dollars a week, and had made only twenty-five dollars for the madhouse exposé, it was a small fortune.

Hence my new, if empty, apartment on West Seventy-Fourth Street. Compared to the furnished room I'd occupied all summer, it was a palace: six large rooms with a private hall, a bathroom with a tub, and a kitchen with a range. There was a common freight elevator in the building for groceries, and a janitor's service was included. The rooms were outfitted with gas chandeliers, steam heat, and fairly decent woodwork. I even liked the wallpaper. All for twenty-two dollars a month—a steal.

And I wouldn't be alone for long. Even before the book deal, I had sent to Pittsburgh and asked—well, told—my mother to sell her house and come live with me. I did it partly out of duty, partly as repayment for all the trouble I'd caused her over the years, and partly because we had been good companions during my months reporting in Mexico.

There was another, less worthy reason as well: I wanted to show up my brothers.

Of my four siblings, the oldest two were both married and employed. But Charlie had remained at Mother's house even after his wife had produced a bundle of joy. And Albert, the eldest of us all—and Mother's favorite—now lived in a fine house of his own in Pittsburgh, yet he hadn't invited our twice-widowed, once-divorced mother to live with him. No, *I* had done that. In New York, no less. Me, the troublemaker. Me, the heck-raiser. Me, the one Albert considered undignified and incapable.

It was petty of me, but it felt so good to throw my money and success in their faces.

However, if I really wanted to show up my brothers and impress my detractors—of whom I had many—I needed to continue making my name. Knowing enough to strike while the iron was hot, I had been on the lookout for another story just as good as Blackwell's Island. I had to keep producing unique pieces for the *World*. Every Sunday that Nellie Bly had her name in print was a victory.

My male colleagues resented my sudden success, which seemed to have struck from out of the clear sky. Few of them rated a byline, and they all thought I got mine simply because putting a woman's name above a story gave it the level of sensationalism that Colonel Cockerill prized.

While I understood their resentment, I dismissed it. They had enjoyed their exclusive "no girls allowed" clubhouse for long enough. They could open the doors to admit just one lone girl. *If they don't like it, well, they can lump it. Nellie Bly isn't going anywhere but up.*

To do that, however, I had to find another story.

I'd gotten some initial inspiration from a passing comment by the *World*'s lawyer. His tip led me to stint of impersonating a woman in search of work to expose the underhanded practices of New York's employment agencies. These swindlers fleeced women by demanding money in exchange for empty promises to find them placement. It wasn't as exciting as my stay in the asylum, but it made for a good story, and it fit all of Cockerill's criteria: it was titillatingly sensational, it had a strong moral component, and—most important—it was exclusive. The piece would run in the *World* tomorrow.

But today, I thought, I need to figure out what to write about next. And it needs to be big.

Fortunately, I got help from the *World*'s readers. I hadn't known what kind of letters to expect after the Blackwell's Island exposé. Praise, I'd hoped. And, yes, there had been laudatory notes from all quarters: doctors, housewives, bricklayers, even a circuit court judge! My favorite was the one that extolled me for giving those madhouse quacks "such a magnificent black eye with such a tiny fist."

On the other hand, there had been many letters condemning me for thinking I knew better than the doctors and nurses, and even some claiming I actually *was* mad and deserved to be locked up for the rest of my life. Though I'd tried to laugh those off, they lingered in my mind far longer than the praise.

However, by a fair distance the majority of the response had consisted of letters telling me where I should investigate next. Within days I'd collected a catalog of outrages that would make a normal girl take to her bed in a faint. Whereas I found them to be full of exciting possibilities. *What does that say about me?* I wondered as I flipped through my stack of recent correspondence.

Amid all the swindles and scandals, one story leapt out to sock me right in the chin. Instantly, I knew what outrage I would be swinging at next.

Babies. Specifically, unwanted babies.

The typewritten letter read:

> *Dear Miss Bly,*
>
> *I have followed your work since the days of your journeys to Mexico, and read with heartfelt sorrow of the plight of the natives of that magnificent but misgoverned country. It was with mingled delight and dismay that I learned of your arrival in New York through your articles on the misdeeds on Blackwell's Island. Delight, that such a smart, insightful girl reporter was present in this metropolis; dismay, that you had to undergo such an ordeal. It is my fervent hope that you never again place yourself in such a dangerous predica-*

ment. *Please count me among your admirers.*

I am writing because I would like to know what becomes of unwanted infants in this city. Without giving details which such a talented reporter as yourself could easily use to identify me, allow me to say that I am a well-off man who, through my church, recently became aware of an unmarried girl who was with child. It was my intention, with the aid of our pastor, to assist the fallen female in a Christian way. We discussed with her the various institutions available to assist her and her expected child. But just as she approached her joyful day she disappeared from our church. Not much later I saw her on the street. As she was clearly no longer bearing, I, meaning nothing but well, congratulated her on her deliverance. First she pretended not to know me. Then she pretended she had never been pregnant at all. At last she said she gave her son away and, cursing me, departed from my sight.

I do not want to invade her privacy, so I will not presume to offer up her name, which is likely an alias. Yet since that chance encounter I have been unable to sleep, worrying about that newborn child. Is he still alive? Where could she have taken him? And how many more children like him are given up each day in this massive city? What becomes of them? Where is it best to donate money? I have asked at my church, and they advise me to give to them. But I am moved to give funds where they are put to the best use. After all, as they say, I cannot take it with me.

I also worry of extralegal means. My wife called on a Mrs. Gray who advertises manicures and vapor baths. She was horrified to discover the house full of new mothers and their babes, and she had the worst feeling that the infants were not there to be cared for.

She was too frightened by her experience there to ask any more questions. We discussed it and decided I should write to you. If there is any fearless ferreter of truth in our Gotham, it is Nellie Bly.

Would you consider looking into the plight of unwanted infants in New York? I can think of no one better suited to the task.

Pitying Philanthropist

My initial reaction to the letter was outrage, naturally. My second was suspicion. *Does he have an ulterior motive?* Yet the writer seemed sincere. He wasn't after this particular woman or seeking her child, which had been my first concern. In fact, I was surprised a man had written this letter—which I recognized as a troubling statement on my opinion of the average male.

Whoever it was that had written, they traveled in wealthy circles. Only the best homes and businesses had typewriters. There had been only two at the *Pittsburg Dispatch*, and even at the *World* there weren't more than a dozen. Mr. Pulitzer claimed he wasn't yet convinced of their longevity, but Cockerill had privately confided the real reason to me: Pulitzer was subject to terrible headaches. It was bad enough when the presses were running, but the clacking keys and ringing returns drove him from his office in an agonized state. So Mr. Pulitzer preferred that his reporters use their Blackwing pencils.

Returning to the letter, I considered the subject matter. I had certainly heard of girls who became pregnant and disappeared, only to return without their child. I wondered how much happier my own sister might be if she were not a mother. Things were not looking well for her marriage. What if their relationship had soured before the birth of Beatrice? Where would Kate have gone?

To Mother, of course. And the family would have seen her through, as we would do if someday she left her louse of a spouse. But what about the girls who couldn't go to their mothers? What about the girls who hadn't married first, but had "fallen" for a man? I certainly knew enough of those. I thought of Ada, probably still toiling away in the smelly cigar factory, letting her hair down at the end of the day to pick up men on the streetcar in order to gain a dinner.

I felt a pang of guilt. I had built the foundations of my career thanks to Ada, and how long had it been since I'd thought about her? Too long. *I am not a good person.*

Whereas the writer of this letter certainly *was* a good person. He seemed genuinely interested in helping—though it did not escape me that it wasn't the women he wanted to help, but rather the children. Because women who gave up their children were abominable, of course. Inhuman. Unnatural. Not worth caring for.

Still, it was a good cause. Better still, it was a good story. And it had a sharp "hook." I had landed a honey with the madhouse, and while I was under no illusion that they would all be such smash sensations, this one felt like it had the potential to build on the legend of Nellie Bly, Crusader for Social Justice. If I did it right, it might just keep my name in the papers and prevent the Colonel and Mr. Pulitzer from thinking my success to be a flash in the pan.

So where do I begin?

As the Philanthropist had already started with the church, I thought I should pursue a different approach. After all, were I in the shoes of an embarrassed girl, the church would hardly be my first stop.

Nor would I turn to the city's many orphan asylums, where babies were instantly sentenced to a lifetime of poverty and deprivation. There was one, I knew, on Blackwell's, not far from the insane asylum. But I would hardly be welcome on the island again, and it was too much to hope that I might repeat my trick of going in disguise. Besides, it might appear to readers that I was a one-trick pony, or had a personal axe to grind. Blackwell's Island was out.

No, I would look for aid from a profession that was not about morality, but rather about science.

I would seek the aid of a doctor.

Of course, my recent experience made me regard doctors with significantly less reverence than I once had. Still, if it were me, that's where I would begin. *So, what doctors do I know? Or rather, do I know any doctors who might be favorably inclined toward me?*

Not likely, I imagined, given the scathing portrait I had painted of the entire medical profession in my pieces in the *World*. Also, the *New York Sun* had labored mightily to tarnish my image with the industry. In their interviews, the rival paper had insisted that the doctors at Blackwell's were all above reproach, and insinuated that I was just a troublemaker looking to make a splash.

Which was true, I supposed.

Wait, though . . .

Thinking of doctors at Blackwell's suddenly brought Dr. Ingram to mind. He had been the only one to show a human interest in the inmates. And he had just flirted with me in a touchingly schoolboy way on the courthouse steps after the grand jury had returned their condemnation of Blackwell's Island. I'd wondered at the time if he'd only flattered me because I had praised him alone among the doctors in that benighted place. But no: the next day he'd sent his card around to the *World* with an invitation to dinner. *Should I ask him about what becomes of these babies?*

Perhaps, but not to start. I'd already used him once to help me with a story. To accept his offer only to prime him for information would be shabby of me. Better to accept after I had done my research. At least it would provide us something to talk about.

Did I just make up my mind to accept a date with Dr. Ingram? It seemed as though I had!

But first, work. I decided to start at the beginning. To that end, on Sunday morning I purchased copies of the *World*, the *Tribune*, and the *Herald*, and swiped a copy of the *Sun* from a newsstand—I refused on principle to give Mr. Charles Dana a solitary cent of my wages.

Sprawled unladylike on the floor of my unfurnished apartment, I read the classified ads. Being young and healthy, I had never had much call to peruse the medical section in any newspaper. So I was frankly astonished as I encountered this obvious example of hucksterism:

DRUNKENNESS or the liquor habit can be cured by administering DR. HAINES' GOLDEN SPECIFIC. It can be given in a cup of coffee or tea, without the knowledge of the person taking it, effecting a speedy and permanent cure, whether the patient is a moderate drinker or an alcoholic wreck. Thousands of drunkards have been made temperate men who have taken the Golden Specific in their coffee without their knowledge, and to-day believe they quit drinking of their own free will. For sale by . . .

And it listed the doctors who sold that slop. I bristled at the thought of a wife spending her own clothes money on the Golden Specific to prevent her soused spouse from wasting all his wages on alcohol. Or in the vain hope of forestalling another beating from a drunken husband. Situations like these were among the many reasons the Woman's Christian Temperance Union was able to recruit so many members.

This spiraled me back to thoughts of my stepfather. My worst night in the asylum had occurred when they'd drugged me with chloral, which triggered a vivid reliving of my final tête-à-tête with him. He'd been as abusive a drunk as I ever hoped to encounter. My mother had tried endless cures and remedies, believing she could fix him, even after the night he pointed a gun in her face.

Making a note to investigate those charlatan cures, I moved on to a slightly more legitimate medical ad:

> DR. SMITH, 2 East 14th St., oldest reliable specialist, both sexes, blood poisoning, skin, ulcers, obstructions, discharges, inflammation, bladder, kidneys, heart, lungs: my method the only one known that cures permanently the worst cases of nervous debility, weaknesses, prostration, trembling, shyness; chronic, unskillfully treated cases solicited. Cures guar't'd. Advice, book free.

Cures for weakness and shyness? He probably peddled some solution of cocaine. Ever since some German eye doctor had discovered its medicinal properties three years earlier, cocaine was the new "wonder drug." And Vin Mariani had been around all my life. Not being much of a wine drinker, I'd never cared for the stuff, and Mother said it made her jittery. But it sold well. Indeed, it was rumored that Vin Mariani was the inspiration for Pemberton's French Wine Coca, which had added kola nuts to the mix. Mr. Pemberton had even created a nonalcoholic version, keeping only the coca leaves and kola nuts. I'd never had it, but I knew people who just adored Coca-Cola.

A similar pledge appeared in the next ad, touting a doctor who catered to "gentlemen only" and vowed to "rapidly cure" their mental and physical prostration. And another one guaranteed to restore "lost vigor and vitality" to weak men and women "suffering from errors of youth, &c."

Errors of youth? That's promising . . . Oh, no, wait. The ad concluded with: "Full treating for home cure of all private diseases mailed free, securely sealed." No, that was no help.

I was quickly becoming concerned at the evident abundance of weakened men. *Who knew so many of the poor dears were so frail?* Though not all treatments were laughable. One advertised treatment by "Electric Belts and Suspensory System." Trying to imagine it, my mind conjured a kind of steam-driven rack.

Reading on—and on—I set some rules for myself. First, I determined to ignore any doctor who did not list their name. Personally, I wanted to hunt them all down and expose them as the frauds they undoubtedly were, but if I were a pregnant girl with nowhere to turn I would crave the comfort of a name.

Second, I'd avoid any doctor claiming to treat a long list of ailments. I'd want an experienced and discreet expert, not someone fishing with a wide net. Also, a long ad meant money, which meant a big fee.

Eventually, I chose to start with an ad in the *Sun*. Of course it would be the *Sun!*

> ALL DISEASES and complaints satisfactorily cured or no charge; either sex; medicine; largest experience, hospital, &c.: London and New York: oldest reliable. Dr. Hawker, 21 West 13th Street: advice free, 9 to 9.

To a girl in trouble, the mention of London would be impressive, offering an air of legitimacy. "Oldest reliable" suggested a gray-haired grandfather with steady hands, and the Greenwich Village address promised the reassurance of a classic Greek revival townhouse or a reliable brick house with large windows, rather than the dilapidated tenements of the Bowery, with drunks and pickpockets and wrecks of womanhood loitering outside.

All of that could have been fine. It was the no-fee-unless-cured promise that rang hollow. To a young girl at her wit's end, it would seem miraculous, too good to be true. Because it probably was.

Wasting no time, I answered the advertisement that very afternoon. It indeed turned out to be a brick building, old but not fashionably so. I entered the vestibule and let myself in. The hall was somewhat shabby, but the doctor's brass nameplate beside the door was shiny and impressive, so I marched up and knocked with my gloved knuckles.

The door swung open and I was faced with a short, dapper man with a bald head. He peered over his glasses at me. "Yes?"

"Dr. Hawker?" I said, leaning into my native Pennsylvania accent, which had somehow fooled doctors and a judge into thinking I was Cuban.

He lifted his brows as if to say, *Obviously*. "Yes?"

Halfway to uttering my rehearsed lie, I spied a mournful young man in the office behind Dr. Hawker. Experiencing sudden confusion, I got caught on my tongue and then decided to make use of my embarrassment. "I want to speak with you. Privately, please."

"Oh, yes, yes. This way," said Dr. Hawker. Stepping out into the hall, he closed the door on the cheerless fellow and led me further down the hall to a back room. "Wait here, I will see you presently."

From the furniture of the back room—a bed-lounge, chairs, cupboard, stove, and bureau—it seemed that the doctor used this waiting room for all his personal needs. I was already considering rifling through the bureau when I noticed there were two other souls waiting there, a man and a woman. *Probably shouldn't, then.*

The pair sat at a little table off to the side. They didn't greet me, so I played the role of timid young mother and, lacking a third chair to sit upon, perched quietly on the edge of the bed-lounge to wait.

The doctor called up each of us in turn—I assumed in the order we arrived. I transferred myself to a chair when it became vacant and was happy to note that I could not hear any of the discussion in the front office. No one would then be able to eavesdrop on our interview.

Soon it was my turn, and Dr. Hawker ushered me into the front room. The floor was nicely carpeted, and the chairs, desk, and medicine case all lent an air of a well-to-do physician.

Dr. Hawker drew his chair close to mine—but not so close as to make me feel uncomfortable—and waited inquiringly for me to begin. Fortunately, I had worked up my story in advance. I had thought of pretending to be pregnant, and even considered arriving with a pillow padding my abdomen, but quickly abandoned any such idea. I could not fake my way through *that* exam. Besides, he might offer medicine to rid me of my imaginary child, and that was not the story I was after.

Instead, I said, "I read your advertisement, and as you say you give 'advice free,' I thought I would come to you for aid. There is a . . . a baby I want to dispose of. Can you help me?"

Bobbing his little bald head, the physician did not appear at all shocked. "Yes. How old is the child?"

"It was born on the fifth of May," I answered, trying to add an emotional throb to my voice.

"Yes. Mm. Pretty big child by this time. Boy or girl?"

I was brought up short. *Why didn't I think of* that *before I came?* "Oh, a girl!"

"A girl? Tch. Too bad. They are very hard to get rid of. Now, if it only was a boy, you would have more chance."

Drat. It was on the tip of my tongue to alter the lie and say, *Oh, I meant a boy!* What a look that would have earned me! Luckily, I kept still.

"The child is healthy? What complexion?"

"Neither dark nor fair," I waffled. "It's rather like me. What shall I do with it?" *It? Her, Elizabeth! Say "her"!*

"The child is yours?" he asked, peering over his spectacles at my skinny form and underdeveloped chest. If I were breastfeeding, this fabled child would be starving.

My heart raced as I imagined a litany of questions I was ill-prepared to answer. So I answered his question with a question. "Can it be done?"

Dr. Hawker leaned back easily, removed his spectacles,

and began cleaning them with his handkerchief. "Yes, it is done daily. Mostly, it is done when the child is born," he said, raising his brows in admonishment. Seeing me suitably chastened, he relented. "However, I can advertise for you. Will you make a full surrender?"

"What is that?" I longed for my notebook and pencil.

He replaced his glasses and gave me a remotely stern look. "You give up the child and never know where it goes or anything more about it. I will do this for you for twenty-five dollars, to pay for advertising and all outside expenses."

"Twenty-five?"

"Is that a problem?"

I told him no, since I wasn't going to be paying it. But for the girl I was pretending to be, that was a month's wages. So, twisting my hands in my lap, I pled with him for reassurance. "Tell me something about such cases. This is all new to me. What becomes of the babies? How can the mothers tell whether they live or die, or are treated well?"

I thought he might lean close, pat my arm, be reassuring. But, no. Instead, he lit a cigarette and blew smoke between us. "After a mother makes full surrender of a babe, she has no way to tell what becomes of it. Of course, it may be ill-treated or reared in the wrong manner, but she has to take the chance," he said, waving his cigarette in lazy circles through the air. Then he shrugged. "We advertise, people reply. We never ask them who or what they are. I know as much about them as I do about you this moment. Many of the women who come for the children are veiled and we never even see their faces. If satisfied, they take the babe, pay their fee, jump into a carriage, and drive away. To where? No one knows."

As if to assure me that no one would ever be able to connect me to the abandoned babe, he continued, "The child has no chance ever to find out who it is. The ones who take it have not the faintest idea who the mother is, either. They have never even seen her."

My mind was whirling. This was not adoption. This was not fostering. This was not even abandonment. These little babies, most of them newborns, were being sold without care or concern for what happened to them. They were human chattel. In a country that had recently fought a war against slavery, it was horrific.

I must not have been able to keep the shock from my features, for Dr. Hawker quickly said, "Of course, there are some women who do not make full surrender, but get me to procure boarding places for the babies. I had a woman who lived on Fifty-Second Street that did all this work for me, but she died a few weeks ago, and I have no one to replace her yet. Normally, I can have a child boarded for four dollars a week. No, the care is not what mothers would give. And what is the death rate of such children? At the very least, eighty out of one hundred."

I sat there blinking, attempting to keep the anger from my face. Scowling, Dr. Hawker stood and crossed to his desk to stamp out his cigarette. "You think it horrible? Well, it's the way of the world. Some women who do not want the expense of a child, and who do not wish to make full surrender, leave them at the Catholic Home on Sixty-Eighth Street, near Lexington Avenue. When the home is not full, a basket is hung on the doorknob at night, and women drop their babies into it. If you are not a Catholic, you won't want to do that," he said, smacking his lips with distaste. "Others give them to the Commissioners, who send them to Ward's Island, where there are eight hundred children. If you dread bad treatment and large death rates, you should see that place!"

One night on Blackwell's, I'd heard the cry of a child born into that wretched environment. Now I pictured a whole other ward, filled with a regiment of nurses like Grupe, charged with caring for babies: refusing to close windows, leaving them in their own waste, denying them food, warmth, human contact. Or like the brutal Nurse Grady, forced to care for colicky infants, growing frustrated, and shaking the children to death—or simply dropping them on their heads. I shivered at the thought.

"Yes," said Dr. Hawker, observing my shudder. "You see it now. Full surrender may not be ideal, but what in life is?

And it is far better than putting your little girl in the care of New York State."

Clearly, he wanted me to choose the full surrender, and he seemed tremendously annoyed that I was not falling to my knees to thank him for the simple, painless solution he was offering.

"You have given me so much to think about," I told him, rising and taking up my bag. "I'll take tonight to think things over. If I choose to make the surrender, I will come back tomorrow."

"With the twenty-five dollars."

"Of course. Thank you, doctor."

He showed me out, and I made it around the corner and out of sight before I halted to collect myself. I was shaking, and not from the chill October air. Normally when I uncovered a good story, I was exultant. But not today. And if past experience told me anything, I was something better.

I was angry.

To the Superior of the Foundling Hospital:
We have arrested a woman for intoxication and vagrancy at 11 this
PM. She has this infant about 3 weeks old. She wanted to destroy it.
So it is not proper to leave it in her charge and even if she were sober,
she is not in a fit state to take care of it.
The child will not live if it does not have nourishment. If you will
take care of it, also the older one until to-morrow, I will then have
them sent to Commissioners of Public Charities.
We have tried to get some of her people to take care of this infant.
They all refuse. I do not know what else to do with these children than
to leave them in your kind protection for this night and by so doing
very much oblige.

Yours Respectfully,
Charles W. Coffry,
St. Patrick's Cathedral, New York

TWO

SEVERAL THINGS KEPT ME UP that night. Chief among them was the fact that I had stumbled upon such an inhuman scheme on my very first interview. Now, I knew I was lucky, but it was absurd to think that luck alone could account for my instant success. That is, unless the practice described by Mr. Hawker—I suddenly had trouble thinking of him as a doctor—was not only common, but generally accepted.

I was also troubled by the fee. Twenty-five dollars from the mother made for a tidy profit, especially as I doubted the money went toward advertising—I liked to think that Colonel Cockerill would have noticed someone placing an ad that read "Baby For Sale. White, Female, Healthy. No Questions Asked." So the "good doctor" was making a modest amount off the desperate mother. *How much is he making from the buyer? What is the going price for a newborn child these days?*

Having slept but little, I set out early the next morning for my second interview. Only when I set foot outside was I reminded of the date: Halloween. The Irish-friendly papers carried tales of fairies and witches, while the more staid ones ignored the holiday entirely. The most lavish commentary came from the *Brooklyn Daily Eagle:*

HALLOWEEN

Away back to the time when Rome was mistress of the world, when the silent sphinx along the banks of the Nile marked a mighty city, dates that welcome presager of winter holidays—HALLOWEEN.

Julius Caesar, Mark Antony, Alexander the Great all ducked for apples when they were boys, no doubt, and perhaps young Caesar picked the bowl with the fatal ashes when he tried his fortune. Halloween is one of those delightfully romantic celebrations of which we have too few.

Suddenly I was transported back to Apollo, Pennsylvania: a child listening to spooky stories, thrilling in being terrified, and searching our old house to find a ghost to befriend. It had been a time for friends, and I felt a vicious pang as I thought of the story I was investigating, of children being raised away from the warmth of family and friends. *What becomes of them? Where do they go?*

It was with those questions in mind that I met with a very different type of healer. First, she was a woman. Second, she wasn't a doctor. Mrs. Conradson's brief advertisement described her as a "Healing Medium" who held hours "from 9 to 9." So, promptly at nine a.m., I approached a large, three-story brownstone house. From the closed shutters and doors, the building appeared to be vacant, and I was forced to ring several times before a German maid appeared to show me into an office on the ground floor.

The room was neat, and surprisingly well-appointed, given the exterior appearance of the brownstone. Similarly, Mrs. Conradson herself was not ill-looking. Perhaps it was the date, but I had come prepared to face a hook-nosed witch. Whereas this lady, while never having been a beauty, was in no way ugly. Straight nose, full lips, clear eyes—if set a little too close together. Her black dress suggested she was a widow, but she wore neither veil nor gloves indoors, indicating her loss was not recent. She kept her uncovered iron-colored hair in a neat bun.

She took my hand as we sat. "How can I help you, my dear?"

"I have a child I want to get rid of," I said bluntly, "without being known or appearing in the matter. Can you help me?"

She nodded sagely. "A boy? Or a girl child?"

"A boy." After all, Hawker had said boys were in more demand.

"How old?"

"Three months."

"And his coloring?"

"Like me. Dark hair, but fair skin."

"Very handsome, I'm sure. Well, my dear, I could certainly arrange for him to be boarded. The cost would be about five dollars a week. But since you're so young and sweet, I'll try to bring it down to four."

The going rate, I thought. Aloud, I said, "No. No, I want nothing more to do with him. I must cut off all connection. It's best for us both."

She patted my hand again in a very motherly way. "I see, I see. Looks too much like his father, does he? Well, my dear, for ten dollars I could get someone to take him off your hands for good and all."

Only ten? Even in crime and immorality, women were paid less than half a man's sinful wage.

I put on a show of relief. "Truly? And he will have a decent family, and a mother who will take care of him? Proper care?"

"Certainly. Very proper."

No dire warnings from Mrs. Conradson. But then, I had asked for the full surrender myself. "How will you find such a family?"

"How do I place them, you mean? I advertise them."

"Where?"

"In newspapers, in certain circles."

Certain circles. *Hm. There must be a code for such things.* "Seeking hopeful mothers," or some such. I made a mental note to ask the Colonel to have a word with the advertising department. "Who answers the ads?"

"Lots of people. Plenty come only through curiosity. Many come in hopes of tracing a lost infant, imagining they see resemblances in the baby's face to a girl they suspect gave up her child. Never fear, my dear, never fear," she assured me. "I always know such people. They ask who the mother is, what she is like, where is she from, if I have any knowledge of the father, and what sort of man visited the mother while she was here. I very quickly show them the door. Those who truly want babies never ask a single question." Mrs. Conradson tilted her head quizzically. "How long have you been here from France?"

France? "I'm from the South. New Orleans."

"Ah, that explains it. I knew you didn't belong here. A true New Yorker would not have to ask so many questions. And I wondered why you kept the child so long. I always advertise the day after they are born. I don't charge anything for placing babies when they are born here. But, as yours was not, I will have to charge you for my trouble. Ten dollars is little enough. And you must bear all other expenses, for I may not be able to place him for a month or so."

"I understand." *Now to find out where they go.* "There cannot be so many women willing to take on such a burden."

"Oh, there are plenty of willing takers," she told me, then added, "it's just that there are so many babies."

The way she said it, so matter-of-factly, chilled me to the bone.

"But what do these women—?" I began.

Now fully convinced I was a yokel, Mrs. Conradson simply cut in to finish my question. "What do they do with them? Ah, that is hard to say. I have known women to get babies repeatedly, but I don't know what for."

Worse and worse. "Who are the mothers?"

"I cannot tell you that. Confidentiality is everything."

"No, I mean, what kind of girls are they? Poor girls? Working girls?"

"Oh, no, never poor girls! They cannot afford it. All come from the middle and higher classes. Not one out of a hundred is a working girl."

That brought me up short. Until that moment, I had only imagined poor women giving up their children. After all, why would a woman who could afford the care of a child give one up? And yet the moment she said it, I knew it was true: a poor woman couldn't afford the fee to be rid of her baby. Only a well-to-do woman had the privilege of freeing herself from motherhood.

"And these wealthy women all want to get rid of their children?" I asked.

"Only occasionally. They generally tell me to get a home and they will pay for the keeping. I have a long list of people who will watch children. The minders mostly live in flats, and keep themselves on the incomes derived from mothers. Sometimes the mothers know where their children are and visit them, but oftener all business is done through me."

"And the child is well looked after?"

She shrugged. "I do not suppose the best care is taken of babies. What can one expect of a woman who may have twelve to care for? If they die, they are buried as the minder's child and no questions are asked."

"Are there really so many babies?"

"Why, my dear, there is no place that can equal New York. There is a doctor who runs a large place on Sixth Avenue for aristocrats alone, and his place is always filled. He keeps all the babies, but I can't say what he does with them. He never knows who his visitors are, and he only asks one question of them, and that is: What should he do with them in case they die?"

In case they die.

"Are there no other places for the babies?"

"There are free homes for children, but if you want the child to live, you won't take the chances there," she said gravely. "And no right-thinking person would trust the Catholic Foundling Home."

"And the mothers remain anonymous?" I insisted, keeping to my role of anxious mother.

"Absolutely. I've had girls come to me who said their homes were only a few blocks away, and no one was ever the wiser. I am the only one who knows them. It is seldom I recognize my guests, and they do not see one another."

Better for her, I imagined, to know nothing. Her deniability was her shield.

"I wish I had known of this place before," I said ruefully, and meant it, though in a very different way than she understood. "Are you often busy?"

Serious and serene up to now, Mrs. Conradson almost chuckled. "My house is never empty. I have only one room unoccupied now. In connection with this, I am a doctor and I give massage and electric baths."

"And the girls who stay here, do their children ever die at birth?"

"Yes, a number do. Either way, the mothers are never here longer than two or three weeks."

Though I did not yet have a definite answer for what became of the babies, I decided I had heard quite enough from Mrs. Conradson. Feigning gratitude, I promised to return with ten dollars that afternoon in exchange for her assurance that the baby's fate would never be traced back to me.

I emerged shaking. *Is it terror? Or anger?* I couldn't tell.

M Y INVESTIGATION WAS DERAILED THAT afternoon by the arrival of my mother from Pittsburgh, with three steamer trunks of clothes and bric-a-brac. I had her room prepared, and after she got settled I planned to take her out for a welcome dinner, with a stop at Newspaper Row to see where I worked.

Equal to my delight in seeing her was my annoyance that she had brought my eldest brother as her chaperone. Albert was oil to my water.

"All hail the pen of Pink," he said as he roamed my apartment. Pink was my childhood nickname. "Shame you can't afford a chair or two."

"I'm being picky," I told him, my arms crossed defensively.

"Sure, sure," nodded Albert knowingly. "Well, if you're thinking of filling it with the family furniture, don't. Mother is splitting everything between Charlie and me." He shot me a grinning glance to see how that landed.

It was a blow, but I wasn't about to tell him that. "I understand. I can afford new things. You and Jane need all the help you can get."

Though Albert kept smiling, by the narrowing of his eyes I knew I had scored a hit of my own. He returned to deriding the spare nature of my apartment, asking if I was trying to create a private haunted house for Halloween.

Mother emerged, freshened up after her trip, and we all went out for an early supper. I spent the three nickels to buy our fare for the streetcar downtown, and guided my guests to the corner of Tenth Street and Broadway, home to the Vienna Bakery.

"Not Delmonico's?" asked Albert. "What, can't afford it?"

"Delmonico's is for tourists," I lied—everybody ate at Delmonico's. But I was trying to sound worldly, and I wanted to give Mother an experience she would adore, and Albert one he would detest. To tweak his nose, I added, "Besides, you wouldn't like it there, Albert. The cashiers are women."

"How very French," remarked Mother.

The Vienna Bakery was not an evening establishment. Arriving just before closing, we ordered a full meal, which I'm sure put the cooks out. But I wanted Mother to experience their famous pink ice cream, which came served with three slices of cake. Being "Pink" myself, I took special delight in sharing my signature desert.

After dinner, Albert said he was off to find a saloon and a hotel. I saw Mother give him money, which bothered me in the extreme. He was married and had a job, yet he continued to sponge off Mother's meager funds. I kept my mouth shut, however, as I led her to Newspaper Row to view the *World* building, where I worked. I may have cried a little.

On the way back home, I told Mother about my current story. "I'm trying to find out more about what becomes of unwanted babies in the city, so I've been answering advertisements aimed at new mothers."

Mother eyed me warily. So did the other women on the streetcar, though more covertly.

I had to laugh. "It's for a story! Really!"

Mother turned to the woman beside her and said, "She's a reporter."

"Oh!" exclaimed the stranger. "Like Nellie Bly!"

Surprised, Mother met my eye and smiled. "Yes," she said, "just like Nellie Bly."

A FTER BREAKFAST THE NEXT MORNING, it was back to work for me. I left Mother to unpack and Albert to explore the city, and started with a call upon a Mrs. Stone. It took a bit of running around to find her, as she used a proxy at her listed address, but eventually we shared the same air. A round, jolly woman, she had a similar sales pitch to Mrs. Conradson, but was far more chatty.

"This being New York, I presume you have plenty of this business to do," I suggested.

"Plenty," she agreed readily. "Why, there is no business that can compare with it."

I could not resist saying, "It seems profitable, this business."

"Oh, yes! The business pays, for our clients all come from the higher classes. Sometimes I know the buyer, but more often not. Sometimes the buyers are particular and want to know that the child is legitimate—born in wedlock, you know. I keep several marriage certificates on hand to satisfy them. They never see the mother, though, nor she them," she assured me.

"It is a blessing there is someone willing to take charge of their babies," I ventured. "Else it would be hard on the mothers, I suppose."

"Oh, child! It would make me sick to tell you what is done by girls who cannot pay to have their babies adopted. I knew one girl, the daughter of a clergyman in Jersey City, who ran away from home and came to New York. After all her expenses were paid, she had not enough money to pay for adoption. When it was time for her to leave, she rolled up a bundle of clothing and, taking her baby, said she was going home. On the way, she smothered the child." She clucked her tongue sorrowfully, as if the tragedy was inevitable. I did not point out that if Mrs. Stone had waived her fee—*Mrs. Stoneheart, more like!*—the lost babe might still be alive.

At the next stop on my tour of the rings of Hell, the dour Mrs. Gollas was perfectly willing to take a baby off my hands for a mere thirty-five dollars. The fee was large, she noted, because of the age of the supposed child.

"I always have children taken away on the first day. It is a great deal of trouble to have older babies adopted," she said.

"Why is that?"

She looked at me as if I had fallen down the proverbial stupid tree, hitting every branch on the way down. "Because women wish to pass the babies for their own, of course, and so they get them young."

"And these women wishing to adopt—where do they come from?"

"All over! I've had them come from France and Germany. They have property that depends on an heir, and want to cheat other relatives out of it, so they buy a child. Of course, in those cases complexion matters. In most cases, in fact."

"Are they all wealthy women?"

"Of course! What would poor people want with them?"

"And does the mother never know what becomes of her child?"

"My dear, even I do not know! I never wish to. Though there was one occasion . . ." Mrs. Gollas grew sly, her eyes carrying the twinkle of someone in possession of the best joke in the world.

"Yes?" I prompted.

Evidently, it was too good a tale not to share. "A short

time ago, a woman gave up her babe, and the parties who
adopted it told me accidentally that they had bought a home
on Long Island. When I told this to the woman, as strange
as it may seem, it turns out they had bought their home
from her father. They would be her neighbors, though they
never knew it. So the woman can see her child every day."
How awful for her, I thought as I departed. Which was
worse—not knowing, or knowing?

IN THE EVENING I POSED that very question to my
mother. We had fallen at once into old habits, chatting
between rooms as I set the table. She insisted on cooking
for me, and had spent all afternoon working to make this
first meal an occasion.

I was grateful to not have to toil at it myself. I was even
more grateful that Albert had taken the afternoon train
back to Pittsburgh, as I didn't know what I would do if
he ever came for an extended stay. *Probably smother him in
his sleep.*

That made me think of the clergyman's daughter and
her little bundle. I related that story to Mother as I finished with the cutlery, and then shared the tale of the
woman with the baby adopted by the unknowing family
next door. As she brought in a tureen of her delightfully
creamy pumpkin soup, I voiced the question that had been
on my mind all afternoon. "Which is worse, do you think?
Knowing, or not?"

"I think it will be worse, in the long run, for her to see
the child every day." Returning to the kitchen, Mother
removed the pork chops from the stove and added a dol-
lop of homemade applesauce. "Time heals the wound of
loss—unless the wound is kept open, festering. I think a
clean break, while painful, would be best."

Fluffing the napkins, I paused, struck by her words.
Mother didn't know it, but that had been my ulterior
motive in coming to New York: a clean break. Not with

a child, but a man. I had fallen in love with a man who was not free to love me in return, and too gentlemanly in nature to allow me to delude myself.

Yet I had failed. After only one kind letter, I was again pining for the Quiet Observer. I feared that wound would fester the rest of my life.

I roused myself as she came in with the plates and quickly took my place. She told me to say grace, and then we set to.

After a few mouthfuls of her delicious holiday soup, I said, "Did you always want to be a mother?"

Mother looked at me quizzically. "Of course. Even as a little girl I imagined having a little girl of my own."

"Oh." I felt . . . I wasn't sure how I felt. Sad. Bitter. Somehow false? An imitation woman.

"I'm not a mother," I began.

"You relieve me," said Mother, eyes twinkling.

"Ha-ha," I said dryly. "Yes. But since you are one, I wanted to ask—could you imagine ever giving up a child? I mean, I'm sure there were days when you wished you could send me back to the store."

"Several! But the stork said no returns." Mother became serious. "No, Pink, I could never have contemplated giving any of you up. Though you must remember, when you were all born, your father was alive and we lacked for nothing. Later—well, I did contemplate finding someone willing to take better care of you than I could. But the Cochrans were unwilling."

"Really?" The children of my father's first marriage had forced us to leave our home in order to secure their inheritance. "I thought you didn't trust them, based on their ill feeling for us." That ill feeling went in both directions.

"Perhaps that, too. Besides, the Cochrans were busy with their own lives." It spoke volumes that she referred to them as "the Cochrans," as if they somehow were real, and we were imposters. It was why I had added an *e* to the end of my name, to define myself, claim my own identity, even before I became Nellie Bly.

Mother blew on the soup in her spoon. "This is about

these abandoned children. You're wondering what kind of mother gives up her child."

Just the opposite, I thought. *I wonder how any woman* keeps *her child.* Aloud, I said, "I think I understand them. They feel guilty that they cannot provide for their little one. On top of which, they're simply afraid of being responsible for another person. They must feel that someone else, anyone else, would be a better parent than they are."

"It doesn't make it right, Elizabeth." Not Pink, Elizabeth. She was making a point.

"No," I agreed slowly. "But it doesn't make it wrong, either. If they feel inadequate to the task, shouldn't they give their place to someone else?"

"They were willing to sin. They should have known the price. Compounding sin with more sin solves nothing."

"They made a mistake. A mistake no man is ever forced to pay for. Yet we expect poor young girls to bear the entire brunt of their error."

"Children are not errors, Elizabeth. They are blessings."

"Not for everyone, Momma. Speaking for myself, I cannot imagine anything worse than being a mother right now."

It came out before I could stop it.

From the look on her face I was sure I had wounded her. So I was surprised when, pausing midway through cutting her pork, Mother said, "I am so grateful I did not have a child with your stepfather."

A fraught sentence. Even the framing was dangerous. She hadn't used Ford's name, nor had she called him her third husband. She'd called him my stepfather, as if he were somehow my possession. Making him *my* fault, not hers. It made me bristle. *She* had married him, after all, not me. But I knew she'd only done so because being the wife of a lout appeared better than being a widow whose late husband had failed to provide for her children. Appearances, of course, could be deceiving. In actuality, it had been much, much worse, and we had all suffered.

But I couldn't say any of that. Two years earlier, while she was my chaperone in Mexico, I'd found out that

Mother carried the blame for Ford as a festering wound. Every word out of my mouth on the subject of marriage, relationships, children, responsibility, or especially money seemed to jab her with a pin. Mother saw me as judgmental and unforgiving.

After our set-to in Mexico, I had trod lightly around the subject of Ford. And it was hardly appropriate dinner conversation. Still, she had broached the subject, so I followed up. "What would you have done if you had? If he had given me a brother or a sister?"

She said something in a voice so low I couldn't hear her. "What, Momma?"

She dropped her cutlery with a clatter. "I said I don't know." She drew a breath, then continued more calmly. "He certainly wanted me to. He used to fantasize aloud about what our children would look like, what we would name them. But I think I knew, deep down, that if I had a child with him I would be tied to him forever. And perhaps that's really what he wanted. He certainly didn't much care for you girls, though he was fairly good with the boys. Especially Albert."

Two peas in a pod, I thought. Albert resembled Ford in so many ways—manipulative, scheming, vindictive, lazy, grasping, and nasty. And he was another man who despised women.

He was also my mother's favorite child, so I kept my opinion to myself.

Rousing herself, Mother wiped her chin with her napkin and began busing dishes. "As I say, I am glad it never happened. I had enough guilt over bringing the five of you into that household."

I wasn't done eating, but I still followed with my own dish. "Was it luck?"

"Was what luck?"

"Not having a child with Ford."

Mother looked at me disapprovingly, though for the question or for using his name I couldn't tell. "Not entirely."

I felt the pressure to change the subject, and so I did, talking of the play I wanted to take her to see on Saturday.

But I could not help wondering if Mother had used the miracles of modern science to prevent conception. Or had she found a Mrs. Gollas in Apollo and procured the means to rid herself of a pregnancy.

It was an unwelcome train of thought, one that would travel faster and faster as my research continued.

A FTER ANOTHER DAY OF INTERVIEWS, I felt I had fairly mined the vein of doctors in the city. Yet one more ad caught my eye:

> DR. MAY—W. 24th, graduate of university, Phil., Pa; 25 years' experience, skillful, safe treatment; one interview sufficient, consultation strictly private.

Inexplicably, I clung to hopes that a fellow Pennsylvanian would have higher morals than these cynical Gothamites. Instead, I found him to be the worst of a terrible lot.

He began by trying to impress me with his credentials, showing me diplomas from medical colleges in New York and Philadelphia, and boasting of belonging to the Board of Health. "And I'm a member in good standing at the Masonic lodge."

By now, my story had altered a little. No longer pretending the child was mine, I claimed to be acting on behalf of a friend. No one cared a fig about the provenance of the mythical babe. They cared only about the fee.

After hearing my tale, Dr. May readily consented to take charge of the child for the modest sum of five hundred dollars! Beholding my shock, he attempted to reassure me. "Believe me, there is nothing you could ask that would surprise me, nor any act that I will refuse to perform! Dr. May? Dr. Will!" Laughing at his own feeble jest, he casually sipped from a bottle of laudanum. "I am the soul of discretion! A physician, you see, is bound not to reveal the secrets of his patients. Once, I was taken to court in a divorce case. It was just another story of a jealous husband and pretty wife in love with her physician. But I refused to reveal anything, and the man lost his case. An insurance company once took me up on a case where a man died of hard drink. I treated him for it, but I would not admit that to them, and so the company was the loser. And I have never, ever testified when a woman arrived in a state of distress after attempting to miscarry on her own. Nor have I reported a woman to her friends or parents for, ah, social diseases."

He took a second swig of laudanum. Seeing me squint at the bottle, he offered it over. When I declined, he said, "Forgive me. This is a very stressful occupation, you understand. And you must not believe what women say about me! They say it about all doctors. I cannot help it if women become excited or aroused in my presence. It's not me! I mean, I'm handsome enough—or so I've been told. No Henry Dixey, to be sure, but still . . . Anyway, it isn't me at all. It's the chemicals we keep here for treating patients! Women are always more susceptible to such things. But I can treat that easily. Have you heard of the Manipulator? Or," he chuckled, "as we doctors call it, Granville's Hammer? It's a wonderful device for calming women down by bringing all their hysteria to fruition at once. Let me show it to you!"

"No, thank you!" I practically shouted, itching to flee. He seemed positively insane. Besides, I had no desire to learn what Granville's Hammer was meant to hit. "I'm only here about the baby."

"Right, right," he said, thumping his palm against his head in what he clearly felt was a comical fashion. "Well, have no fear on that score. I'll be silent, to my grave. Women always trust me in the end. They know that once they pay, I'm bound not to tell on them. And they're bound not to tell on me. Do you have the money with you? No? I understand, that's a lot of money to carry about. But give me something, anything. Two bits, as a retainer."

I paid him his twenty-five cents just to leave his presence, shuddering as I departed. *No more doctors!*

"I'M SO GLAD YOU AGREED to come out, Miss Cochrane," said Dr. Ingram, sitting across a table from me at the Old Homestead Steakhouse.

I had returned his note and agreed to meet him for dinner on Wednesday evening. He chose the place, famous for its oversize portions. Diners had taken to carrying home their uneaten meat to feed to their dogs. If asked, the restaurant even provided little "doggie bags" for that purpose.

The place was expensive, I knew. But he had ordered for us both, so I hadn't gotten the opportunity to scan the prices. He was being extravagant for our first meal together out in the world: roasted onion soup, wine, and two massive sirloin steaks that each looked bigger than my head. I wondered if my appetite had finally met its match.

"It was kind of you to ask me, Dr. Ingram," I said. "And very forgiving. After all, our initial acquaintance began with a lie."

"I wonder, is a lie a sin if it's told to uncover a greater truth? And please, call me Frank."

I nodded, then chuckled. "You'll have to forgive me again. I find myself in a quandary over what I want to be called."

He raised his brows in genial interest. "Oh?"

"Yes, it keeps coming up. I like having a private life as Elizabeth Cochrane. After all, that's been my name for twenty years." *Twenty-three. Another lie.*

Ingram smiled in understanding. "But most of New York knows you as Nellie Bly."

"Yes. And here you are, someone I met as Nellie Bly—"

"Nellie Moreno, actually. Or was it Nellie Brown?" We both laughed.

"You see what I mean! My worlds are overlapping, and the lines are blurred. All of this is to say, I don't know if I should like you to call me Elizabeth or Nellie."

"Which one do you think of yourself as, in your head?"

I considered. "When I'm angry with myself, or disappointed, I'm Elizabeth. When I am who I want to be, I'm

Nellie."

"Then, with your permission, I'll aim for your better self. Hm." His cheeks dimpled as he had an idea. "Nellie is short for Penelope, isn't it? What if I called you that?"

That surprised me. *Another alias!* "Why not?"

We talked for a time about the grand jury investigation into Blackwell's, and the rumors he'd heard since departing. "Nurse Grupe has been fired, and Nurse Grady left of her own choice. I heard she moved to Vermont, where her name is less infamous."

"Not for long, if I have anything to do with it," I said, brow clouding.

"Oh?"

"Oh! I haven't said. It's going to be a book!"

He offered congratulations. "Your great feat, immortalized for all to see."

"Yes. And then everyone will know how they treated the patients."

Dr. Ingram shook his head. "And none of us saw it."

"Because you weren't looking." It was a true statement, one that did not relieve him of responsibility. Nor, I hoped, did it sound too condemning.

I asked him how his new private practice was taking shape, and he spoke of the trouble of finding the right house out of which to work, and the difficulty of gathering clients. "It does help to have been singled out for praise by New York's latest crusading hero. Heroine. I'm thinking of taking out an advertisement that reads 'Nellie Bly Approved.'"

We chuckled over that. Cutting off another thin slice of the fat steak, I paused before raising my fork to my lips. "I have a confession to make."

"I knew it. You are insane after all."

"Yes," I agreed after swallowing my next bite. "I'm mad for this steak. What's your prognosis?"

"Hopeless."

"Hopeless?"

"Yes. Udderly incurable."

I stared.

Ingram blushed. "Sorry. Couldn't help myself."

"Puns are the lowest form of humor. Don't take my word for it. I know Bill Nye," I said, referring to the humorist who had started out West and now wrote for the *World*. Saying I knew him was a bit of a stretch. I'd *met* him once. In passing.

"I've read his work. What's he like?"

"You know how people from the West always seem like they're lounging? That's him. I think cowboys are required to slouch."

"Some in my profession think bad posture is a sign of moral weakness."

"Pardon me if I don't think much of your profession."

"I cannot blame you. You've seen us at our worst."

"I certainly thought so. But this week I seem to have really scraped the bottom of the barrel. Which brings me to my confession. As we're speaking of doctors, I have to admit I wanted to talk to you about some I've recently met."

He winced. "Oh, dear. Another black eye to my profession, courtesy of Nellie Bly?"

"I'm afraid so. Listen." As I related how I had spent my week, Ingram grew first pensive, then actively regretful. I finished by saying, "I'm afraid my morality must be skewed. This seems so very common, so unremarkable, that I feel *I* must be wrong to think it so very wrong. You're a doctor. Tell me, is this wrong?"

He laid down his knife and fork—evidently I'd killed his appetite. "Of course it is. You don't need me to tell you that."

"Yes, but is it common?"

He compressed his cheerful lips into a flat line. "I have never encountered it, but one hears stories."

"But why do these rich people not adopt from an orphanage?" I demanded.

"If I had to guess, I'd say it's because children in an orphanage are older."

"What has that to do with anything?"

"Women who desire children want them from birth. They crave complete influence over the child. One never knows what experiences a boy has had, how he has been raised, shaped."

"And this is America," I grumped. "The land that craves everything new. Right down to electric vapor baths."

"Good Lord, I hope you didn't try one," said Dr. Ingram at once. "I doubt their efficacy."

"Of course I didn't." *Not yet.*

"I'm relieved to hear it. So Nellie Bly is going to crusade for lost children now. A worthy cause."

"Thank you. But I have one qualm."

"What is that?"

"I . . . I've been thinking about it since talking it over with my mother. Clearly, this trade is so common that eradicating it would be a lifetime of work. In another life, I'd take up finding decent, respectable homes for every one of these children. All I can hope now is that my story puts these shameful doctors out of business and serves as a warning to all the others out there engaging in this trade."

"I hope so too," said Dr. Ingram. "Now tell me your qualm."

I crinkled up my face as I tried to find the words. "I guess I'm wondering if I'm in danger of harming these women."

"Which women? You mean the mothers?"

"Mothers who don't want to be mothers, yes."

"How do you mean, harming them?"

"By removing the option of giving up their child."

"Would that be so awful? That they would be forced to raise the child they gave birth to?"

I don't know quite what my face conveyed, but Dr. Ingram saw he had erred. He raised his hands. "Don't mistake me! I'm not judging them. I simply think a child has his best chance with his mother."

"You don't believe in adoption?"

"Of course I do. But if these women didn't sell their babies, perhaps more unwanted orphans would be adopted instead."

It was an interesting point, I had to admit, but one that did nothing to help these unwilling mothers.

"If it eases your qualm," he said, "realize that you cannot entirely remove that option. Desperate women also abandon their babies at police stations or on church doorsteps. The only thing you'll be removing is the fee."

"Yes," I said, nodding slowly. "If a woman wants to give up her role as a mother, she shouldn't be forced to pay for the privilege."

Dr. Ingram didn't like that much. *I suppose most people wouldn't. Especially men.* Society deemed it unnatural if a woman did not desire to be a mother. My own mother felt just the same. After all, what else were girls good for?

Nellie Bly, aberration. Unwomanly. A botch of nature. A monster.

Sister Irene,

The child in question is indeed an object of charity. The mother is in danger of death, is but 15 years of age and without means of providing for the child. The child has been baptized in this church.

Yours in Christo,
Rev. William Hogan

Sister Irene,

This poor girl Margaret Hanigan is much to be pitied, and owes all her misfortunes to drunken parents. I have always believed she is not vicious, and any thing that can be done for her will be a charity.

Your servant in our LORD,
Wm. Everett
Pastor, Nativity Church

THREE

HAVING FINISHED WITH DOCTORS, I decided next to turn my attention to other types of medical ads. The author of the letter that had started me on this dismal tour of travesty had stated his wife had visited a manicurist who gave "vapor baths."

I started with a parlor on West Sixteenth Street. This was the occasion of my first professional manicure. I'd only ever had my little home manicure kit with its file, under-nail picks, cuticle pushers, buffers, and snips—as well as button hooks so I didn't have to break a nail on the dozens of buttons I dealt with daily. Only, I always forgot to use it. And I was never able to achieve that perfect almond shape to my nails, with the little crescent moon down at the base of the cuticle.

As my manicurist worked, I felt a giddy delight thinking of the fit Colonel Cockerill's secretary, Mr. Marsh, would have when I asked for reimbursement. But such a shine! I almost resented the gloves that would hide my perfect fingernails. *Nellie Bly, lady of society!* It made me laugh aloud.

Before leaving, I made a discreet inquiry and, to my relief, the manicurist promptly turned me out. I visited four more parlors along Sixteenth Street and all the women I met seemed shocked by the nature of my visit. It wasn't lost on me that it was the medical professionals who were engaged in this trade, while the working ladies of lower social standing displayed better character.

Having found manicurists to be legitimate, I decided to rattle the doorknobs of some bath houses. I had never before experienced a vapor bath, but in contrast to venturing a manicure, trying one prompted mixed feelings. You were forced to sit completely naked on a stool inside a barrel-like metal contraption, with the doors closed around you, leaving only a hole at the top for your head to poke through like a groundhog sniffing the air. Then, beneath the thing, a fire created the desired type of bath. Before reading the sign outside my first stop, I had no idea there were so many varieties: Dry Steam, Vapor, Alcohol, Oxygen, Perfumed, Mineral, Sulphur, Hot Springs, Russian, and Turkish. The sign also proclaimed that the vapor bath "eradicates disease by natural means, and is recognized as thoroughly scientific by all learned physicians. It cures without medicine—destroys germs, eradicates impurities, equalizes the circulation, and relieves internal organs. Nature's Mode of Restoring Health and Beauty!"

Even before Blackwell's I'd have had little interest in taking off my clothes and being locked in a barrel with only my head peeking out. Since my experience there, I'd repeatedly woken in a sweat after reliving some of the worst nights locked in my cell, especially the chloral episode. My heart started to pound at the thought of again voluntarily giving up my liberty and risking my flesh.

Yet it was the risk that had so excited the imaginations of my readers. And it was the risk that had so thrilled the Colonel and Mr. Pulitzer. Risk was the foundation of Nellie Bly's reputation. So I marched in and took a vapor bath.

To start with, it was like being back in Mexico, where women congregated in communal baths to gossip and relax away from men. But here there was no sense of community, only isolation. I stripped naked behind a screen and, wrapped in a towel, clambered into the lopsided box of galvanized iron. Inside stood a stool and a footbath, both wired to a battery. The doors were closed around me, leaving me protruding from the neck up like a waxen head at Madame Tussaud's.

Vapor was then generated by means of a spirit lamp underneath a small galvanized dish of water placed in front of the footbath. While the vapor built up, electricity was applied by means of a sponge electrode. Protected by partitions from the other bathers, I was encouraged by the matron to thoroughly rub this electrified sponge over the surface of my body, thus closing the circuit with the stool and footbath.

In essence, I was to give myself an electric shock while surrounded by steam. It sounded horrifying, and I was made to recall the promise of a hysterical paroxysm thanks to Granville's Hammer. For a long minute my common sense did battle with my curiosity.

Curiosity won and, shielded from view, I hesitatingly touched the electrode to my knee. An exciting little hum of vibration rippled across my skin and made me laugh aloud. Keeping my mouth firmly closed, I applied the sponge to my elbow, then my tummy, my hip, and—at last—the very tip of my left breast. I flushed as I did so, feeling daring and not a little naughty. I decided there and then to exclude this adventure from my official reporting.

I spent two days visiting ten matrons who advertised either medicated, vapor, or electric baths. Eight out of the ten were in the habit of taking children for money. "The whole year does not bring a slack week," one told me, adding, "Of course the majority die. Which is fortunate, in a way. Is it supposable that there are enough rich families to adopt them all?" A helpless waif more or less, a death more or less, it mattered not to them. It was only "there's a new kid come" or "there's another kid gone."

"But if they live, what becomes of them?" I persisted. "If not the rich, who takes them?"

They all shrugged, knowing only two things for certain. First, that supply was greater than demand. Second, only the well-off could afford their fees.

I was no great shakes at economics. But as I understood matters, a surplus of a thing should drive the price down, not up. So if all these babies were indeed being sold, then it seemed there had to be an unmentioned demand from somewhere.

But if there was a flaw in the system, these women refused to see it. If these unwanted children were all being reared in wealthy homes, where was the harm?

MY FINAL STOP WAS THE Mrs. Gray mentioned in the letter that had started me down this awful road. As I climbed two flights of narrow, dirty stairs, I heard the wail of newborns.

Mrs. Gray was a frizzed-fringed white-haired woman with a stoop and the beginnings of a hump on one shoulder. She was also cagier by far than any of my other unknowing interviewees. She demanded my whole story up front, and only when she was convinced I was genuinely trying to off-load a child did her guard relax. "One has to be careful, you understand. There are so many schemes going around. I had a woman come here the other day that acted as if she were one of those female detectives you read about. I gave her no information. You never know when you will get caught up.

"I had a woman come to me one day and say that her husband threatened to leave her if she did not part with a child she had previous to the marriage. She got me to take the child and put it in a home. She paid me well and paid the child's board, visiting it every week, while the husband thought she did not know where it was. He even hired a private detective to shadow her, and yet her secret remained hers alone. The child is now seven years old, and—yes? What is it?"

A young woman had come in carrying a bundle. Placing it in my arms, she unwrapped the front and for the first time all week I looked upon an actual child. A girl. Her little eyes squinted at the sudden light, and she lolled her head to one side.

"No, no," said Mrs. Gray to her employee. "This lady is here to give up a child, not take one."

"It's all right," I said. Staring down into that open, innocent face, I cannot say why I was so stricken. Perhaps it was because until this moment the children were all theoretical, living in my imagination alongside the cherubic dimpled babe I had invented. But here was a tiny thing, unable even to support her own head, little gummy mouth grasping at the air for a breast or a finger.

I had never in my life desired to be a mother. But at that instant, I was tempted to take that child and run.

M Y DEADLINE WAS FAST APPROACHING, and I felt I'd barely scratched the surface. I had enough to outrage the public, but as yet I had no answer to the question that had launched my investigation: what becomes of unwanted babies in the city? With barely enough time for one more research trip, I decided not to visit any more doctors or bath houses, but instead one of those institutions where babies were known to be taken in. Wanting to avoid a return to Blackwell's, I recalled Dr. Hawker warning me against the Catholic charity house, so I decided to see how they fit into this puzzle.

Thus, I took the train to the Upper East Side to visit the New York Foundling Asylum. It was on Sixty-Eighth Street near Third Avenue, just a block north of the newly established 19th Precinct of the New York City Police Department, with a fire station right next door, its watchtower rising over all.

But the police precinct and firehouse on Sixty-Seventh Street were dwarfed by the massive, sprawling complex on Sixty-Eighth. The Foundling Asylum was made up of five interconnected buildings: a maternity ward, a west wing for girls, a central administrative office, an east wing for boys, and a children's hospital.

Climbing one of the double sets of stairs tucked against the front of the building, I entered the imposing seven-story administrative office. The building had electricity, and quite possibly its own generator, as I could hear the hum of power in the wall sconces.

The nun at the front desk was working on her fingernails with a kit. *A nun with a manicure? Why did that bother me? Surely even a sister of Christ was allowed to make herself feel pretty. With her hair hidden all day long, what else is left?*

Perhaps I was bothered that she hardly looked up at me, even as I related my errand. Nowhere near compassionate, she seemed utterly bored. No longer pretending to be shy about the situation, I asked whom I should see about giving up my friend's child.

"I will only make arrangements with the mother," answered the sister tartly. "If she gives us the child, she never sees or hears from it again. We only take full surrender and no one can know where they go."

Again the full surrender. "Would she have to pay?"

That made her glance up for a fraction of a moment. "Donations are welcome, always."

"But there's no fee?"

She lost interest and returned to her nails. "Of course not."

I studied the imposingly massive wooden doors to the left and right, both carved with scenes from the crucifixion. "May I look around?"

"No. The public is not allowed beyond those doors."

"Who is in charge of this place?"

"The founder, Sister Mary Irene." She might as easily have been speaking of the Lord Our God.

"May I speak to Sister Mary Irene?"

"No, she is very busy."

"Not too busy to speak to a woman about the safety of a child, surely."

Huffing at me, the manicured nun rang a bell on her desk. A little girl of perhaps six years dressed in a uniform dress and apron came racing around a corner and curtsied. "Take this young woman"—Sister Manicure was not going to call me a lady—"up to Sister Irene's office and wait there with her until Sister Irene arrives."

Of course. I might steal something. Or, more likely, go pawing through records.

The little girl led me up four flights of stairs to a neat, spare office with a large desk, a wall of books, and a globe of the world. The child offered me a seat and I took it on condition that she sat with me as well.

"What is your name?" I asked her.

"Elsie."

"Mine's Elizabeth. Do you live here?" She nodded. "Do you remember for how long?" She shook her head. "Do you know why you came here?"

"I'm a charity girl."

"What do you mean? You do charity work?"

"I'm only a poor charity girl. I ain't got no home." She pronounced *ain't* as *haint*.

Understanding her meaning, I felt a sudden kinship for her. "Are you an orphan?"

"I s'pose I am. I was sick, and Momma couldn't afford a doctor."

Her mother gave her up? "Sick with what? A fever?"

Elsie's hand moved involuntarily toward the collar covering her throat. She caught herself and her hand dropped. "I couldn't breathe good."

"Couldn't breathe *well*, Elsie girl," came a voice from the open door. "Couldn't breathe well."

Sister Mary Irene was a thin-faced woman with almost no lips. Yet a smile always lingered at the corner of that thin mouth. Despite a left eyelid that drooped a little, she had the most keenly piercing gaze I could remember feeling. Broad of shoulder, broad of hip, she carried the lilt of her Irish accent like a lead pipe in a silk sleeve.

Sister Irene took us in as she crossed to stand behind her desk, framing herself in a large window. "Baby posture, please, child. Sit up straight. That's better." Her eyes rested on me. "And who have we here?"

"Elizabeth," said Elsie.

"A fine name," said Sister Irene. "But I think she's here to talk over a private matter, child. Kindly return to Sister Mary Agnes and tell her I said you have done well." With a curtsy to me and to Sister Irene, Elsie scampered out.

"Baby posture?" I asked.

"Babies do not slouch." Sister Irene studied me for a moment. "I understand you're here about a child. But if it is not your own, we cannot help you. We only offer aid if the mother asks, or if a figure of authority intervenes. How else are we to know the child hasn't been removed against the mother's will?"

"But you take in children left at your door."

"At such time there is no other choice." She eyed me carefully. "You aren't truly here to give up a child. You're here to find one. Was that why you were pestering wee Elsie with questions?"

"I'm not here looking for a child," I assured her. "I'm here looking for all children."

That gave her pause. She sat. "Go on."

"I'm a reporter for the *New York World*. A reader sent a letter asking what becomes of unwanted children in the city. I've spent a week discovering the most awful, inhuman practice of doctors forcing women to pay to be rid of their children. And since I was warned against this place, I thought, before I wrote my article, I should see it for myself."

Her eyes narrowed. "What was your name again?"

"My pen name is Nellie Bly."

I saw a flush warm her Irish cheeks. "Well, well. Blackwell's Island. You did a whole lot of good for those poor girls. Are you here to expose us as well?"

"I'm here for the truth."

"Ah, that we have in abundance. If you like, I'll give you free license to roam this building. But I'd prefer you be accompanied by one of us if you're going over to the maternity ward or the hospital." She smiled. "For the protection of the patients, not the hospital. We have nothing to hide."

"I'm pleased to hear it," I said, trying not to show my skepticism.

"To be clear, though, I want none of these poor women named and shamed in your story. They're suffering enough." "That seems fair." I pulled out my notebook. "Where should we start?"

"Follow me." Rising, Sister Irene paused, and I felt the full weight of her frank-eyed gaze. "How old are you, Miss Bly?"

The question startled me, but I'd been lying about my age since my first editor had knocked three years off it, and the answer was automatic. "Twenty."

Releasing me from the pincer grip of her eyes, Sister Irene led me out for my tour. "And you've only recently come to New York, is that right? For how long?"

"I arrived here at the start of the summer."

"It is impressive that you've accomplished so much in such a short time." We started silently treading down the carpeted stairs. "But it means you have no knowledge of what it was like here in the fifties and sixties. Homeless children were an epidemic, a plague on New York."

"How many were there?" I asked.

"Official estimates were ten thousand. If anything, they erred on the conservative side. We reckoned there were close to thirty thousand homeless children here. Out of a population of half a million."

The numbers staggered me, and I struggled to jot them down as we turned toward the boy's dormitory. We walked quickly, probably so that I did not have a chance to linger in study of the children.

"Back then, children did whatever they could to survive. They sold matches or, if they were lucky, newspapers— that's where the newsboys originate. Often they would band together to form gangs. You've heard tell of them all by now, I'm sure." I nodded. "Well, it was unsupportable. There was a time when Tenth Avenue was known as Misery Row."

As she talked, we passed a set of ground floor school-rooms where uniformed boys were learning their letters. I felt sure that to them *this* was Misery Row. *They have no idea how fortunate they are.*

What would have become of me if Ford had pulled the trigger on Mother? I've always felt like an orphan, but what if I'd become one in fact? If my sister and I had both become charity girls like Elsie? I would have been lucky to end up in such a place as this.

And yet, I would have rebelled. Pink, the troublemaker. Now, and always.

Sister Irene continued at her brisk pace. "That's where a young theologian from Yale enters the story. Do you know the name Reverend Brace? He saw that almshouses were not enough, and struck upon the notion of shipping orphans off to other parts of the country."

"You're talking about the Orphan Train," I said.

"You've heard of it?" she asked, pleased.

I had. "It uses the railways to carry homeless children off to work on farms and such, yes?"

"Just so. Mr. Brace founded the Children's Aid Society to find places for children all across America, and runs it to this day. A godly man, for a Calvinist."

As Sister Irene continued, we passed along the connecting corridor to the children's hospital. "Trouble is, the majority of the children he sends off are aged eight or more. Few frontier families desire newborns—a farm needs hands, not another mouth to feed."

"Is that how you—?"

"Yes. After the war, I saw how many children were in the streets. Wee ones, barely talking, and yet off on their own with no one but other children to look after them. Certainly, the almshouses could put a roof over their heads and offer a modest meal. But there was no education, and no provision for infants at all. So nearly twenty years ago, Sister Mary Theresa and I hired a house on Twelfth Street. That was the start. We put a little cradle in the vestibule. I'd read that back in the Dark Ages, churches would have a small revolving door about the size of a bread box. A woman would put her child into it, ring the bell, and depart. The sister within would turn the door and take in the child without ever setting eyes upon the mother. They called it the 'foundling wheel.' We started our own version of that in the vestibule. We began with just five dollars to our name. After outfitting ourselves to care for the children, there was nothing left. We ate our first meal kneeling on the floor, with newspaper for our tablecloth."

"And now you have all this."

"All this?" Sister Mary Irene eyed the cramped conditions of the ward with consternation. "Sure and it's hard-hearted not to be grateful, but it's not near enough. There are so many children to look after. Come and see." She led me into the children's ward.

Here was an army of tiny beds, some open, some with rails, and some—the smallest—canopied with gauzy white material. A handful of nurses in gray gowns with white aprons and mobcaps moved between the beds, carrying moist towels or fresh diapers.

As we walked between rows of beds, I said, "How many— what should I call them, patients? How many patients do you have here?"

"Across this campus we have over one thousand seven hundred souls at present, mothers and children. Mostly children."

"What kind of cases do you get here?"

"All kinds. Influenza and diphtheria are the worst."

"I read there was quite an outbreak of diphtheria this summer."

"Yes, a terrible one." She smiled, and saw my questioning look. "Two years ago, when we had such cases, we lost so many to the disease. This summer, thanks to one of our doctors, we lost none."

"He found a cure?"

"Not a cure, exactly. But a treatment. Have you ever seen someone suffering from diphtheria?" I shook my head. "It is quite dreadful, and especially dangerous for children. Their wee faces grow distorted by their terrible struggles to simply breathe. Their eyes bulge, their faces become masks of agony, and they're racked by feverish convulsions. Their wheezing breaths sound like sick locomotives moving at a snail's pace along the track. It's the swelling in the throat. Children die from it more often than adults.

Smaller throats, you see?"

We ascended to a second floor, where there were more private rooms—I supposed for children suffering worse maladies. Sister Irene spoke the whole time without getting winded, whereas I was laboring for breath to keep up.

"Well, time was a doctor had to cut an opening in the patient's throat and place a tube in to bypass the swelling and allow air in. You asked Elsie about her throat?"

"She said she couldn't breathe good. Well," I hastened to correct myself.

"She wears the high collar to hide the scar of her tracheotomy. But just last year one of our doctors, Joey O'Dwyer, invented a whole new way to keep sufferers breathing without having to cut them at all. He calls it 'intubation,' which is just as it sounds. He places a rubber tube of his own design down the patient's throat, which keeps the air flowing no matter how swollen the throat becomes." Sister Irene beamed with pride. "Now there's a story for you. The *Brooklyn Times* ran an article about his invention this summer, and he plans to present his findings in medical journals next year. And don't go taking against him because he worked with children on Blackwell's for a time. He's doing the Lord's work, and he's the toast of the College of Physicians and Surgeons."

"What a marvel!" I said, asking her to repeat his name. "Dr. Joseph O'Dwyer. He'll be a rich man soon."

Sister Irene's halo of pride grew even more radiant. "Oh, no. He refuses to patent it. He gives it freely to the world for the benefit of humanity. A true healer."

I made appreciative noises, and indeed I was impressed by such altruism. But it did occur to me that had he chosen to patent his device, the proceeds might have gone to this institution, helping even more children in New York.

A twinge of guilt tweaked my heart. I had always wanted to be rich. Never again scrabbling for funds, never again being forced to choose between eating and paying rent. *And here's a man who's both brilliant and genuinely good, passing up a fortune in favor of humanity.* I knew I myself was not so selfless. *But,* I promised myself, *when I become rich, I will use it to the benefit of others.*

OUR TOUR LOOPED BACK THROUGH the main building and headed into the girl's dormitory, taking us past the schoolrooms that mirrored the boys'. Only here, uniformed girls aged five or so were learning to sew, not read. I knew that, had I been a child here, I would have tried to sneak into the boys' lessons. I wondered for a moment if any of these girls wore pink stockings in order to stand out, as I had. But they had no mothers to indulge them.

"Do you ever run out of beds?" I asked as she took me through their sleeping halls upstairs.

"Often."

"What happens then?"

"The Orphan Train is one place they can go if they're old enough. But there are so many under the age of six or seven, we must keep in constant contact with other foundling homes in the area. For example, just now there are eight hundred children schooled at the Five Points Mission, of whom about half are resident orphans. Another two hundred at the Howard Mission and Home for Little Wanderers on Riverton. The Newsboys' Lodging House on Duane Street houses about two hundred boys regularly and feeds up to a thousand on holidays—not this week's frivolous one, but Thanksgiving, Christmas, Easter, the like. Tompkins Square Lodging House keeps about a hundred and fifty. The Howard Colored Orphan Asylum holds one hundred and ten Negro children. I don't have the current figures for the Hebrew Orphan Asylum on MacDonough, but last month they had over seventy."

When I finished scribbling that down, I looked up in astonishment. "You hold all that in your head?"

"I must," said Sister Irene with a proud sniff. "They send me the figures each week so I'll know where there are openings. So many families don't wish to be aided by a Catholic, you see. Prejudice exists in every human heart, in one form or another. And we try to honor the mother's wishes. Often we send them to one of those. But, God willing, we can find them homes before then."

"I'm told older children are more difficult to place. And girls are less desirable than boys."

"Oh, there's truth enough in all that, if a woman's looking for a family. But they only want newborns. It is easier to find a home for a three-year-old dog than a child of the same age. On the other hand, there are far too many places interested in taking a child on to labor around the house or the farm. Young girls are often taken in to be maids, not daughters. Time and again those girls are back here themselves in just a few years, giving birth to their own waifs."

The dreaded word that had been lurking at the edge of my mind all week came bubbling up again. How naïve I had been, thinking that slavery had been eradicated for all time. It only took on different forms.

As we approached the maternity hospital, Sister Irene paused to warn me not to stare at these girls, and absolutely forbade me to question them. "They are here because they have no place else to go. They must feel safe and unjudged, as they receive enough of that from the world at large. If we are to save their souls, we must first make them feel they have not fallen beyond redemption."

Upon entering, we heard a wail of pain from an upper floor. As no one evidenced any dismay, I assumed one of the patients was about to be delivered of her burden.

There were no beds on the ground floor of this ward, lest peepers attempt to see the women here. I imagined angry husbands whose wives had abandoned them, or furious fathers seeking their fallen daughters, standing on their toes in the flower beds outside to peer in the high windows.

Upstairs, I saw partitions between the beds, offering a modicum of privacy. Screens were the token of illness, usually placed around a dying patient's bed. Here there were screens around every single bed. Instead of being delighted at the prospect of giving life, these women were being treated as if they had a fatal disease—which doubtless they themselves believed.

So many swollen bellies and swollen eyes. "I would like to hear some of their stories."

"I told you that is not possible. Even if one girl is willing, her neighbors might take it into their heads that their own anonymity was in danger."

"But how else can I relate to my readers the circumstances of the women who give up their children? They cannot be allowed to think them all harlots or girls of easy virtue."

Sister Irene considered. "Come back to my office," she said at last.

When we had returned to her sanctum, she opened a cabinet drawer and leafed through filing folders. She emerged with a dozen letters.

"These are just a sampling of the notes left with the infants in the foundling wheel, or at parish churches or police stations. You may not publish these. Though they are not recent, they might be used to track down children who have gone on to live lives of happiness. Or to discover that a child left in our care has died. Neither outcome is desirable. But if you want a sense of why women give up their infants, this will provide some answers."

I thanked her and sat down to read:

Dear Sister,

Alone and deserted, I need to put my little one with you for a time. I would willingly work and take care of her but no one will have me and her too. All say they would take me if she was 2 or 3 years old, so not knowing what to do with her and not being able to pay her board, I bring her to you knowing you will be as kind to her as to the many others who are under your care, and I will get work and try hard to be able to relieve you of the care when I can take her to work with me. She is only 3 weeks old and I have not had her christened or anything.

No one knows how awful it is to separate from their child but a mother, but I trust you will be kind and the only consolation I have is if I am spared and nothing prevents and I lead an honest life that the father of us all will permit us to be united.

A Mother

Dearest Sisters,

This offspring is the fruit of a brutality on the person of this poor but decent woman and to cover her shame and being too poor to support the children, there are two from her husband, she is obliged to resort to this extreme measure. The child is not yet baptized.

Sisters,

The little baby which was left in the crib on last night, if you for the love of God and his holy mother you will keep it for me I will give anything you require. Her father is a wicked Orangeman. I told him it was dead because I want to have her raised a Roman Catholic and have nursed out. I will pay all the expenses.

Will you, dear Sisters, remember a kind mother's heart? If I do not see her again I will never do any good on this earth. I work at dressmaking for a living. My husband gives me but a third of his earnings because I am a Roman Catholic. Write to Father Farrell, Barclay Street Church, state circumstances to him. Pray to the Blessed Virgin for me to help me through.

Sister Superioress,

I am a poor woman and I have been deceived under the promise of marriage, I am at present with no means and with out any relatives to nurse my baby. Therefore I beg you for god sake to take my child until I can find a situation and have enough means so I can bring up myself. I hope that you will so kind to accept my child and I will pray god for you.

To the Sisters of the House,

Necessity compels me to part with my darling boy. I leave him, hoping and trusting that you will take good care of him. Will you let some good nurse take charge of him and will you try to find some kind hearted lady to adopt him and love him as her own while he is young that he may never know but what she is his own mother? It would break my heart to have him grow up without a mother to love and care for him. God only knows the bitter anguish of my heart in parting with this little dear, still if it costs me my life I am obliged to give him up.

He is just from the breast, he has been sick with his bowels, they have not been right for a long time.

I have cried and worried over him so much that I think my milk hurt him. I think a change of milk with good care will make him well soon. I got these things thinking I could keep him but as I can not they may be of use to you. I shall always take an interest in this Institution.

He is 4 weeks old. Will you please to remember his given name and if he is adopted, request that they will not change his name; so that at some future day, if that name should be asked for, you will be able to tell what became of him or where he is. Perhaps you will think me very particular, but if any mother will take it home to her own heart and think how she would feel to have her dear little boy torn from her breast, I think they would excuse me.

This is the last time I can speak of him as mine, and if in years to come if I could hear that he had a home and kind friends, I could die in peace. On the other hand, if I should never hear, it would haunt the day of my death. Please excuse all that you think is not right but for God's sake remember the last request of a heart broken mother.

Dear Sister of Mercy,

I tied a little turquoise locket round his neck, please let him wear it. Please, oh please keep him in the Asylum! Please, for God's sake grant my request—you will never have to regret it—My poor dear daughter may come to reclaim her child in a short time and she is so agonized for fear she may get a child not her own. I am going to send a little chain for his neck on which to put the little locket that is now round his neck. Please permit it to be done. I cannot understand how a simple number can ever identify a child.

you can keep the Baby or put it in the street or not for i will not pay for it

Kind Sisters,

you will find a little boy he is a month old to morrow it father will not do anything and it is a poor little boy it mother has to work to keep 3 others and can not do anything with this one it name is Walter Cooper and he is not christen yet will you be so good as to do it? I should not like him to die with out it his mother might claim him some day I have been married 5 years and I married respectfully and I did not think my husband was a bad man I had to leave him and I could not trust my children to him now I do not know where he is and he has not seen this one yet I have not a dollar in the world to give him or I would give it to him I wish you would keep him for 3 or 4 months and if he is not claimed by that time you may be sure it mother can not support it I may some day send some money to him do not forget his name.

Sister,

Please take this child under your care and save a poor girl from despair.

Enclosed find $10.00. I will send that sum every month. Please name the child Martha.

This little baby is not christened call him Theodore Walters I leave him here because I cannot keep him and I want him brought up a catholic two protestant ladies want him but they cannot bring him up a catholic

I, Mary Burns of the City of New York and born in Ireland, twenty-four years of age, having been delivered of a female child and being unable to support or maintain the same, do hereby relinquish and forfeit all my right title or claim to the above child to the New York Foundling Asylum for them to support and take care of the same as long as they deem proper. The name of the child is Mary Jane Burns but has never been christened.

Mary Burns
X (her mark)

TEARS IN MY EYES, I thanked Sister Irene and was shown out. Reaching the street in front of the Foundling Asylum, I decided to walk a ways before taking a train. I needed to clear my head.

As I walked down Lexington Avenue, I was startled to see traffic being delayed by five dozen little girls in blue dresses and nearly a hundred boys in blue coats. They were all in line, holding hands as they crossed the street. These were not students. These were orphans, coming to attend classes at Sister Irene's school.

How have I never before noticed how many there are? Prior to today I would have smiled and thought how cute they all were, never realizing they were orphans.

When I had written the letter to the *Pittsburg Dispatch* that ended up landing me my first job as a reporter, I had signed it "Lonely Orphan Girl." I had always felt orphaned after the death of my father. But I had never lost my mother, nor my immediate siblings. I was not a charity girl.

These were *true* orphans, with no one in the world.

Someone had to do something.

THAT NIGHT, AFTER DINNER, AS I sat at my desk with my notes to write my article, I found myself stalled.

Due to the lack of chairs, Mother was sitting at the dining room table, working on a present for her granddaughter Beatrice. She must have heard my noises of frustration, and her voice echoed around the empty apartment as she asked, "Pink? Is something wrong?"

"I'm stuck," I said in disgust.

"On?"

"This story. How to write it."

"The babies? I'd think your outrage alone would carry you along. You've certainly had enough to say about it since I arrived."

"That's just it. I've never had trouble being angry."

"At least you admit it," she muttered.

Ignoring this jab, I pressed on. "Up to now, outrage has fueled my career. But now I can't locate it."

"Really?" Her voice was redolent with surprise.

Rising from my little desk, I joined her at the dining room table. "Don't mistake me. I'll have no trouble penning a scathing exposé on each and every one of these so-called healers who make a profit peddling human beings."

Mother set down her needlepoint. "Then what's the issue?"

"I don't know . . ." I began. "First off, I'm not sure I'm answering the question in the letter. Yes, I can expose the middlemen, the baby brokers. But I'm no closer to discovering what actually happens to the babies. I mean, every one of these charlatans assured me they go to wealthy families. Yet . . ."

"Yet?"

"Yet the cavalier way in which these doctors spoke of infant deaths keeps me wondering."

"Very well. What can be done to find a more definite answer?"

I shrugged. "The only way I can think of is to hire a Pinkerton detective, or else draw in another reporter to watch these places and help me follow any woman leaving with a baby."

"Why not do it, then? It is a lack of money, or time?"

"Not money. Time, yes. And . . ." I trailed off.

Seeing the reluctance in my expression, Mother hazarded a guess. "And you're not certain you want an answer?"

"It's not that," I said, wishing it were. A delicate sensibility was a far nobler trait than the one I was harboring. "This is a Nellie Bly story. I have to do it myself, or not at all."

"I see," said Mother neutrally. "And is your reputation more important than their lives?"

"Of course not!" I snapped, though in my heart I had been accusing myself of that very thing.

An oppressive silence dropped between us. Eventually, Mother took up her needlepoint again, a clear sign that she assumed the conversation was over.

"The next obvious step," I said, as if I hadn't been unconscionably rude, "is to pose as a buyer. See how it works from the other side."

"And end up with a baby?" she asked, eyes still on her work.

"Hopefully things wouldn't get that far."

Mother's mouth was pinched. Then, relenting, she sighed and looked at me once more. "Do you have enough material for a story now?"

"On the baby sellers? More than enough. Three columns' worth."

"Then it seems to me, Elizabeth, that you can undertake both those options at a later date."

I nodded, still gnawing my lower lip.

Having believed she'd solved my problem, Mother frowned. "What's really bothering you?"

"The mothers."

"The mothers? What about them?"

"To shine a light on Dr. Smith, Mrs. Stone, and the whole pack of them . . . I'll have to discuss the mothers."

Mother sighed in understanding. "And you're having a hard time doing that."

"A very hard time. Each time I start to write about the mothers, the same thought keeps bubbling up: if I shut down these baby brokers, where will desperate women turn? What right do I have to remove this clearly needed escape for women burdened by motherhood?"

"Is their plight your responsibility?"

I smiled wanly. "It's Nellie Bly's responsibility. But so is exposing the frauds."

"I see. Quite a double-edged sword."

"At first I thought this was a poor woman's issue. I have always felt for poor young women. Do you remember my first assignment as a reporter?"

"The factory girls," said Mother.

"Yes. I attempted to humanize them, make them less Mary Magdalene and more plain Jane. I tried to show that poverty is not a moral failing."

"And you wanted to do that here?" asked Mother. "Elizabeth, child abandonment is wrong."

"Yes, Mother. Believe me, my flesh crawls just thinking of those orphans. And yet . . . and yet, you didn't read those letters. What choice does a poor woman have? Is she not at least attempting to give her baby a better life?"

"I thought you said it was only well-off girls purchasing their freedom from motherhood. Doubtless to keep their reputations pristine. You have sympathy for them?"

"I'm as surprised as you," I admitted. "Normally, I wouldn't hesitate to castigate them publicly for it. But somewhere along the way I began to see, in them, the same desperation the poor girls feel. It isn't necessarily a fear of shame that prevents a teenaged Astor or Vanderbilt from being a good mother. Some girls simply are not ready to be mothers."

"Something they should have considered before falling for a man," replied Mother tartly.

"Not every girl who becomes pregnant has a choice, Mother. Wealth does not make women less vulnerable to men." Unable to argue that truth, she nodded reluctant agreement. "And even for the girl who does, does she deserve to be punished for twenty minutes of pleasure—assuming it was a pleasure. Men are not made to suffer a lifetime for a momentary satisfaction."

"In a fair world, they would be," said Mother, and I saw a dark flash in her eyes.

"Yes. And in a fair world, every child would be wanted, provided for, loved. But that's not the world we live in. Thank heavens for Sister Irene and the Foundling Home. It's not ideal, but it's at least clean and well-run. I tell you, I feared it would be another Blackwell's. Instead, I discovered people genuinely trying to do good in the world. Only they're overwhelmed by the demand."

"Perhaps your story will bring them new donors. What you told me of their discovery of a treatment for diphtheria is astonishing. You could write a whole article about that."

I shook my head. "That's not a Nellie Bly story."

Mother studied me closely, then shook her head a fraction. "So you won't write about any of it?"

"Oh, I'll write about it! I'll expose the criminal sale of newborns, name every shameful doctor, and laud the Foundling Home. But," I said, making up my mind on the spot, "I will say nothing—*nothing*—against mothers who give up their children. I don't have the right. After all," I said softly, "in the war with life, these women have already made the full surrender."

WHAT BECOMES OF BABIES

NELLIE BLY

What name awakens such universally tender feelings as that of "baby"? Last week some philanthropist wrote to THE WORLD to suggest that I try to find out what becomes of all the baby waifs in this great city. Not the little ones who are cordially welcomed by proud parents, happy grandparents and a large circle of loving relatives, but the many hundreds of babies whose coming is greeted with grief and whose unhappy mothers hide their little lives in shame. Unhappily there are hundreds and hundreds of them, but it is an impossible task to tell what their fate is . . .

Monday morning found me furiously tapping my foot as I rode the elevator up to the *World's* newsroom. Clutching the Sunday edition, I stormed to Colonel Cockerill's office. His secretary protested, but I elbowed past the bow-tied gatekeeper and burst into the smoke-filled glass cage.

On Saturday the Colonel had been delighted with my discoveries. "Bly! This will be a terrific goddamned piece. It'll have the city matrons in a lather and the churches chattering. Well done!"

Now he puffed on his cigar as he surveyed me with raised brows, sensing the storm coming toward that oversize head of his. "Yes, Bly?"

I was shaking with anger. "You cut half my story!"

"Needed the space." He flicked ash onto the Oriental rug.

I nodded at the ash-covered rug. "I hope it catches on fire."

He grinned slyly. "Never has yet. The Chinese are devils, but they make fine goddamn rugs."

"You cut everything about Sister Irene and the Foundling Home!"

"Not true. We kept the part about the nun giving herself a manicure."

"You made them seem as bad as all the rest!"

The Colonel puffed, then blew smoke into the air over his head in a perfect ring. "The *World* has to walk damned carefully around Catholics. Can't be seen as being too favorable."

"Is it favoritism to tell the truth? It's the one place I visited that's doing lost children any good!" A thought struck me. "Wait. Aren't you Catholic?"

He shrugged. "Raised one. But my religion is newspapers, Bly. And this paper has a history. You weren't around for the election in '84. Goddamn slaughter. Pulitzer thought Cleveland was sunk. But then the Republicans said something at a rally for Blaine. Announced they were with him because no dad-gummed way were they going to support a member of a party born of 'rum, Romanism, and rebellion.' Romanism was their downfall. Blaine didn't rebuke them, which let Pulitzer rile up the goddamn Catholics so much that Cleveland won after all."

"So the paper was pro-Catholic."

The Colonel wagged a finger in the air. "Ah, but a paper *can't* be pro-Catholic if it wants to grow. Especially as there's a rumor out that Pulitzer's mother was a Catholic."

I blinked. "I thought Mr. Pulitzer was Jewish."

"Oh, he is. It's why we can't print stories too favorable to the Jews, either. That's just it. He straddles the dang-blasted fence, a foot in each camp. In every camp."

"So we bias our reporting to show we aren't affected by our biases?"

"In a nutshell, yes."

"Even if it means hiding the truth?"

"We're not hiding a blessed thing. We aren't lying. We're just not telling the whole story."

"But they're doing good work!" I protested.

"I'll make sure they get a nice mention around Christmas time. Charity plays damned well at Christmas—no one will object." He stubbed out his cigar. "Look, Bly, don't lose sight of the goal. Outrage sells papers. You've named half a dozen dad-blamed doctors who buy and sell babies. Babies! That's one hell of a story. Everyone knows about orphan asylums. Hell, that place Hamilton's widow set up has been around since the start of the century! It's not goddamn news."

Seeing the mulish set of my jaw, he took a different tack. "Think of it this way. You want action? Action only comes from outrage. Give people a problem, let them stew until they're absolutely boiling over. *That's* when things get done. But if you offer a problem *and* a goddamn solution, everyone figures the problem is solved. It's not *their* problem, after all. Imagine if you'd finished your report on Blackwell's by talking about another asylum that was doing their work perfectly. Do you think there would have been half the outrage? Not fucking likely!"

I couldn't help myself—I gasped. The Colonel appeared startled at his own profanity. Then he steeled himself. He wasn't about to apologize. After all, he'd once shot a man who dared argue with his editorial choices. Yet he was clearly flustered at having used such language before a woman.

He chewed his lip beneath his enormous moustache while I tried to find a counter-argument. He must have thought I was shocked at his language, not his opinion of the job of a newspaper.

"You did good work," he told me in a grudging tone while avoiding my eye. "It's a helluva story." Lifting a paper, he straightened up. "And I have your next assignment. Right up your baseline. Paper box factories."

"Excuse me?"

"The girls who work in paper box factories. They say they're practically slaves. Earn as little as a buck fifty a week. Ten bits. Mistreatment by the owners, unsafe work spaces, dangerous materials. And they're all women. I want you to do what you do best—infiltrate one of these places and rake them over the coals."

"What about the babies!"

"What about the women who *have* the babies, hm? Think of a girl working at one of these goddamn places. How can she support herself, much less a child? Do you think that if they were paid a fair wage they might not give up their little bundles?" The Colonel shrugged. "You can quit the paper if you like. Go and become a nurse, look after a hundred babies." He looked me in the eye. "Or you can stay here and make a difference."

It was unfair. Cruel even. After just two months, he knew exactly how to goad me.

"Congratulations on the book, by the way," he added.

I left his office with the assignment in my hand, unsure of what I felt. Before this story, whenever I'd completed an investigation I'd been able to put it from my mind, instantly eager for the next one.

But in the days that followed—and the weeks, months, and even years—this would be the story that most haunted me. I would often think of that one child I'd held in my arms, wonder how old she was, what she was like, what kind of life she lived. I'd wonder what could have become of her had I paid less attention to Nellie Bly's future and more to hers.

In that story, a seed was planted. I had no desire to be a mother. But I swore to myself that, should the time come when I needed employment in this cruel world, a time when newspaper reporting was not enough, when I had money and stability, I would do something for the orphans of the world.

Someone had to.

FIN

AFTER WORD

This particular story comes directly from Bly's second piece of reporting after her sensational Blackwell's Island story. I was pleased and horrified in equal measure to find the actual ads for the doctors she referenced, and to research the vapor bath craze that was gripping the city at this time.

This is the first of a series of shorter stories I plan to write based on Nellie Bly's articles. My aim here is not to regurgitate her pieces—her own writing remains the best source for her thoughts and opinions. So often her choice of subject matter speaks for itself, especially as she became famous enough to choose her own assignments.

Instead, my goals are threefold:

First, I want to flesh out her stories beyond the two or three columns she was allowed for her reporting, placing them in a larger context.

Second, I want to put her into the story as more than the plucky, pretty girl reporter she often presented herself as being. I want her full life to inform her reporting, as it surely did.

Third, the issues and ills she chose to report one hundred thirty years ago are ones that we, as a society, have not yet properly grappled with. Unwanted children, lack of support for poor mothers, demonization of women for having sex with no corresponding ire for their equally culpable partners, pregnancy through sexual assault or coercion, religious discrimination—sadly, none of these are strangers to us today. Telling friends about this story, I found their outrage became palpable. As Nellie herself recognized, and as the Colonel makes plain, change cannot come without outrage.

What drew me in is what she chose not to address in the piece—the mothers. While she exposed the quacks and hucksters, she was entirely silent on the question of mothers giving up their children, to the point of not even trying to interview them. It's just my opinion, but I think she did not want to expose them to further criticism. She goes out of her way to point out that most of the women giving up their children were from rich or middle-class homes. As ever, there was a way out for girls of means, even if it was criminalized. Societal scorn was reserved for poor women.

I also found it interesting that the mercenary doctors warned her against the Foundling Home, which pioneered modern adoption practices and still exists today. Bly herself visited it, but makes no mention beyond Sister Mary Manicure at the front desk.

I wasn't content to leave it there. After researching this story, I very much wanted to introduce readers to both Sister Irene and Dr. O'Dwyer, who each contributed so much to our modern world. And I wanted to shine a light on the many circumstances in which women gave up their children.

All of those letters are quite real. Thanks to the New York Historical Society and the Orphan Train Museum for access to that sampling of records.

This story sets the stage for Bly's later actions. Toward the end of her life, she did indeed do something about orphans. Returning to America after reporting on World War I from Austria, she found herself without the fortune she had amassed over her life. That's a story in itself. But arriving in New York, she was homeless, with only the contents of her suitcase as her worldly possessions. Fortunately, she still had friends in the newspaper world, so she took up residence in a hotel and began to write. Her articles, however, were very different. She did some reporting, yes, but she also became something of an "Agony Aunt," the forerunner of Dear Abby. She encouraged her readers to come to her hotel with their problems, and filled the empty bitterness of her many losses and reverses of fortune by helping others.

Chief among her concerns was placing orphaned children with good families. She devoted the rest of her life to that end. She also worked to find employment for mothers and fathers so they could keep their families together. She was tireless and quite bullheaded about it, often crossing horns with the officials who saw her amateur meddling as dangerous. But she was Nellie Bly! In her weekly articles she was bringing attention to an enormous problem, especially for children orphaned by the Great War.

She was still herself, of course, and took every opportunity to trumpet her altruism. Never shy to self-promote, even at the age of fifty-five she still had herself drawn as her young self, avoiding photographs when she could help it.

One of the reasons I adore her so is her incredible mixture of daring and vanity, how she campaigned for social justice while tooting her own horn. She was a hell of a woman. As I've taken to saying, the real Lois Lane never needed a Superman.

While it's poetic license to speculate about the effect this story had on her, I have the advantage of looking at her whole life from end to end. She exposed many social ills, unmasked many frauds and monsters, especially in the two years following her Blackwell's Island exposé. That was the period of her very best reporting.

But, of them all, I do think this story had the greatest effect on her. Or perhaps it was merely her first glimpse at a need that the Great War would bring into sharper focus.

The plight of orphaned children—a fitting cause for a Lonely Orphan Girl to champion.

I've fudged the timeline a little here. At the end of my novel *What Girls Are Good For*, I have Nellie's mother arrive after Bly sends a letter to Erasmus Wilson. Though I didn't put the date on that letter, it was written November 13, 1887. But I have Mary Jane appear just after Halloween. This isn't just because I enjoy their interactions, though I do. In a story about mothers giving up their children, I thought it was important for Bly to have her own mother to use as a sounding board.

For this print edition, I've included two articles by Bly. The first is the article that inspired this story, *What Becomes Of Babies?* The second was Bly's follow-up/sequel story from two years later. Following the enormous scandal of Eva Hamilton, wife of Alexander Hamilton's great-grandson, in which she kept purchasing babies to replace the one she had told him was his that then died, there was a renewed interest in the sale of babies in New York City. This time Bly posed as a buyer, attempting to purchase a newborn. That article is entitled, simply, *Nellie Bly Buys A Baby*.

Oddly enough, the story of Eva Hamilton inspired Bly to write her second novel, *Eva The Adventuress*, which was published in serialized form in the pages of the *New York Family Story Paper* by her book publisher, Norman Munro. The first installment of that tale was published December 22, 1889. Seeing how Bly interviewed Eva Hamilton in early October, 1889, she must have been incredibly inspired to finish this novel, as at the time it was published, she was already over halfway around the world in her race to beat the fictional time set by Jules Verne.

Huge thanks to my editor, Robert Kauzlaric, for helping me hone and shape this story—and for designing the gorgeous cover as well!

The next short(ish) story sees Bly take on another societal ill still with us today—lobbyists—as Nellie Bly travels to Albany, NY to trap the notorious Edward Phelps, the self-styled "King of the Lobby."

Following that is my next full-length Bly novel, entitled *Stunt Girl*.

Nellie Bly will write again.

Ave,
DB

WHAT BECOMES OF BABIES
NELLIE BLY

THE NEW YORK WORLD
NOVEMBER 6, 1887

HUNDREDS AND HUNDREDS OF LITTLE ONES GIVEN AWAY YEARLY

NOT THE PETTED DARLINGS OF THE RICH, BUT THE INFANTS BORN TO
SHAME—THESE ARE THE ONES THAT ARE GIVEN INTO ALIEN HANDS—
REGULAR TRAFFIC IN NEW-BORN BABES—A MONEY-MAKING TRADE IN
HUMANITY

What name awakens such universally tender feelings as
that of "baby?" Last week some philanthropist wrote to THE
WORLD to suggest that I try to find out what becomes of all
the baby waifs in this great city. Not the little ones who are
cordially welcomed by proud parents, happy grandparents
and a large circle of loving relatives, but the many hundreds
of babies whose coming is greeted with grief and whose
unhappy mothers hide their little lives in shame. Unhappily
there are hundreds and hundreds of them, but it is an
impossible task to tell what their fate is.

However, here is a condensed account of my studious
inquiries in this direction. I took several Sunday
newspapers and made note of many of the medical and
manicure advertisements. The following is the result:
Dr. Hawker, of No. 21 West Thirteenth street, has a
suggestive advertisement. I thought from that he might
know something on the subject I wished to investigate, so
I called on him. The door opened in response to my knock,
and well-dressed, short man, with a bald head, looked out
over his glasses at me. I saw a young man in the office, so I
said, with a blush not at all assumed: "I want to speak with
you privately, please."

"Oh, yes, yes," he said, stepping out into the hall and
closing the office door; "step this way. Wait here, I will see
you presently."

He opened the door and I entered a back room. It was
already occupied by a man and a woman. From appearances,

the bed-lounge, cupboard, table, kitchen-stove and bureau, I think that room answered the purpose of the entire house. No one spoke, so I sat down on the lounge and took in my surroundings. The front office, into which I was soon ushered, was vastly different from the room in the rear. The floor was nicely carpeted, and the chairs, desks and medicine case all helped to lend the air of the office of a well-to-do physician. The doctor drew his chair close to mine in a confidential manner and waited, inquiringly, for me to begin. My position was a delicate one, and I knew it. So I said: "I read your advertisement, and as you say you give 'advice free,' I thought I would come to you for aid. There is a—a baby I want to dispose of. Can you help me?"

WHAT TO DO WITH IT

"Yes. How old is the child?"

"It was born on the 5th of May," I answered, with a gasp.

"Yes; pretty good child by this time. Boy or girl?"

"Oh, a girl!" (I hadn't thought of this before.)

"A girl?" too bad. They are very hard to get rid of. Now, if it was only a boy you would have more chance." I got a little quaky by this time, and I almost felt like assuring him that it made no difference to me, that really if boys were easier to bargain for it might just as easily be said a boy. Luckily I kept still.

"The child is healthy?" I nodded my head. "What complexion?"

"Neither dark nor fair," I replied, as I couldn't tell the complexion of a babe I had never seen. "What shall I do with it?"

"The child is yours?" he asked.

I was almost stunned, for I feared next he would ask me questions I could not answer without more invention than I was capable of. "I would like it disposed of without any questions being asked. Can it be done?"

"Yes, it is done daily. It is mostly done when the child is born. However, I can advertise for you. Will you make a full surrender?"

"What is that?"

"You give up the child and never know where it goes or anything more about it. I will do this for you for $25; you to pay advertising and all outside expenses."

This was soon agreed on. I did not hesitate at $25 when I was never going to pay it. "Tell me something about such cases. It is all new to me. What becomes of the babies and how can the mothers tell whether they live or die or are treated well?" I asked, aiming for the news I was in search of.

"After a mother makes full surrender of a babe, which is done at the place it is born, she has no way to tell what becomes of it. Of course, it may be ill-treated or reared in the wrong manner, but it has to take the chance. We advertise and people reply. We never ask them who or what they are. I don't know as much about them as I do about you this moment. Many of the women come veiled and we never even see their faces. If satisfied they take the babe, pay their fee, jump into a carriage and drive no one knows where. The child has no chance ever to find out who it is. The ones who take it have not the faintest idea who or what the mother is; they have never even seen her.

"Of course there are some women who do not make full surrender, but get me to procure boarding places for the babies. I had a woman who lived in Fifty-second street that did all this work for me, but she died a few weeks ago, and I have no one since. I can have your child boarded for $4 a week. No, the care is not what mothers would give. What is the death rate of such children? At the very least eighty out of one hundred. You think it horrible? Well, it's the way of the world. Women who do not want the expense of a child, and who do not wish to make full surrender, leave them at the Catholic Home in Sixtieth street, near Lexington avenue. When the home is not full, a basket is hung on the door-knob at night, and women drop their babies into it. If you are not a Catholic you won't want to do that. Others give them to the Commissioners, who send them to Ward's Island, where there are 800 children. If you dread bad treatment and large death rates you should see that place!"

I pretended that I had some love for the imaginary child, and really I did have, so I said I should take the night to think it over, and if I decided to relinquish it I would return on the morrow.

BOY BABIES BETTER THAN GIRLS

Mrs. Conradsen
Healing Medium. Hours, 9 to 9
West 15th st.

So read the next advertisement on my list. I had no idea who she was or what, but somehow the notice seemed to suggest that I would not apply to her in vain. She lived in a large, three-story brownstone house, which had the appearance, from the closed shutters and doors, of being unoccupied. I rang the bell repeatedly before I was shown into the presence of the woman, who was not ill-looking. My first story had been such a success that I decided to repeat it, with a slight difference. As the doctor said girls were hard to get rid of, I determined this time it should be a boy, and so have every chance there was.

"I have a child I want to get rid of, without being known or appearing in the case. Can you help me?"

She then asked the age, health and complexion of the baby boy. Apparently she was satisfied, for she said she could board him out at $4 a week for me. When I told her it was necessary that I cut off all connection with the child, she said for $10 she would get me someone to take it. She noticed my accent and she asked me how long I had been from France. I told her I was a Southerner and she said she knew I did not belong in New York or I would not have to ask so many questions on the subject.

"It seems odd for you to keep the child so long," she said. "I always advertise them in about a day after they are born. I do not charge anything for placing babies when they are born here, but, as yours was not, I will have to charge you $10 for my trouble. That is little enough, and you must bear all other expenses, for I may not be able to place him for a month or so. How do I place them? Well, if the mother makes a full surrender, I advertise them and lots of people answer. Plenty come only through curiosity and many in hopes of getting a trace of news.

"Sometimes they imagine they can see resemblances in the baby's face to one they suspect. I always know such people, as they ask who the mother is, what she is like, where from, if I have any knowledge of the father, and what sort of a man visited the mother while she was here. I very quickly show them the door. Those who want babies never ask a single question.

WHAT BECOMES OF THEM

"What do they do with them? Ah, that is hard to say. I have known women to get babies repeatedly, but I don't know what for. Who are the mothers? They are never poor girls, but all come from the middle and higher classes. Not one out of a hundred is a working girl. Do they get rid of the children? Only occasionally. They generally tell me to get a home and they will pay for the keeping. I have a long list of people. They mostly live in flats, who keep themselves on the incomes derived from mothers. Sometimes the mothers know where their children are and visit them, but oftener all the business is done through me. No, I do not suppose the best care is taken of babies. What can one expect of a woman who may have twelve to care for? When they die they are buried as the woman's child and no questions are asked."

"Are there many babies?"

"Why, my dear, there is no place that can equal New York. There is a doctor who runs a large place on Sixth avenue for aristocrats alone, and his place is always filled. He keeps all the babies, but I can't say what he does with them. He never knows who his visitors are, and he only asks one question of them; that is, what should he do with them in case they die. I have had girls come to me whose homes were only a few blocks above here and no one was ever the wiser. It is seldom I know my guests. I have no desire to know. They do not see one another. I charge from $6 a week to $25. Do I have plenty? My house is never empty. I have only one room unoccupied now. In connection with this I am a doctor and I give massage and electric baths. There are free homes for children, but if you want the child to live you won't take the chances there. Yes, a number of children die at birth. The mothers are never here longer than two or three weeks."

I had all the news I wanted from her and so I bade her a friendly good-by, promising to bring the babe and pay her $10 for its disposal in any manner, so that I was left entirely clear of all connections with it. She asked me no personal questions.

In West Sixteenth street I called at several manicure parlors, but they were found to be legitimate, as far as I could ascertain, although very few of them seemed at all surprised at the nature of my visit. From an advertisement of Mrs. Stone's I concluded she could give me some valuable information as to what became of all the babies. I asked the woman who made her appearance if she was Mrs. Stone. She said no, that the advertisement was put in for a regular practicing physician of Brooklyn. I wanted the address, but she said she was not allowed to give it, but if I would return in a few hours she would ascertain if I could see the party.

A BROOKLYN "HOME"

I got the address on my return, and I went away over to Howard and Monroe streets, Brooklyn. A commodious frame house, surrounded by an ill-kept lawn, stood directly on the corner. It proved to be the one I wanted. From all indications the house was but recently occupied. To the woman who answered to the name of Mrs. Stone, I repeated my oft-told tale, and asked her prices. She could not think of having the child adopted for less than $50.

"I presume you have plenty of this business to do," I suggested.

"Plenty; why there is no business that can compare with it."

"It is a blessing there is some one to take charge of the babies, else it would be hard on them, I suppose," I suggested, in hopes she would venture some information. "It would make me sick to try to tell you want is done many times by girls who have not enough money to pay for having their babies adopted. I knew one girl, the daughter of a clergyman in Jersey City, who ran away from home and came to New York. After all her expenses were paid she had not enough money to pay for having the child adopted. When she was able to return home, she rolled up a bundle of clothing and, taking her baby, started saying that she was going home. On the way she smothered the child. That was the last of it.

"What do I do with the babies? Well, I advertise one as soon as it is born. I never allow the mother to even see its face. Sometimes I know who takes the child, but more frequently I do not. Some people are particular and want the child born in wedlock, so I have several marriage certificates on hand to satisfy them. They never see the mother, or she them. We know nothing of the child after it is taken away. Oh, yes, the business pays, for it is only people of the higher classes who are our patients."

"Mrs. Stone, if babies die while in your care, is it difficult to obtain a burial permit?"

"No, it is very easy. We always retain a physician who never asks any questions, but writes out the burial permit according to our instructions. No, we never give the correct name, but assume any we wish. I seldom know who my patients are. If a patient dies she is buried under the name she gave me. In the Potter's Field? Certainly. It is as easy to get a burial permit for a woman as for a child."

I promised to take the baby to Mrs. Stone the next day, and to sign a paper to the effect that I would never inquire after the child after the time I gave her $50 to dispose of it.

A MONEY-MAKING TRAFFIC

The next advertisement was that of a man who proclaimed himself "ladies' physician," in Sixteenth street. He advertised under the name of Morgan, but the plate on the door bore the name of Dr. Clarke. However, I asked for Dr. Morgan and was told that he was in. The general appearance of the house bespoke good business. Dr. Morgan grew very confidential when he found that I would not hesitate at any price, so the child was taken out of my hands. I had by this time a very tender feeling for this imaginary child. I had lessened his age, as most of them complained it was too old, and I had changed its complexion. I had long ceased to pretend it was my own. It now belonged to a friend of mine. This was a more comfortable position for us. My mind pictured it one of these handsome, dimpled baby boys we read about, and I occasionally felt a mild surprise that the mother could part with it. One's imagination is a wonderful thing when one once gives way to it.

"What becomes of all the babies?" I asked earnestly.

"Most of them die," he replied, "and those that live are given to women who advertise that they will take them. What becomes of them then, no one knows. They procure full surrender and so no one has the right to ask. Or it is very easy to say that some one adopted the child, but they don't know who. It all depends on the mother. If she is willing to spend money she can get a home for it."

Fully eight out of every ten who advertised medicated, vapor, electric or any sort of baths were in the habit of taking children for money considerations. What do they do with them? Is a question unanswerable. They all say that the entire year does not bring them a slack week. Of course the majority of children die, but is it supposable that there are rich families enough to be adopted daily without ceasing? Every one said that only the rich adopt the babies. If it is only the rich, then the supply must be greater than the demand.

The gentleman who wrote to THE WORLD said that his wife called on Mrs. Gray in Sixth avenue, who advertises manicure and vapor baths, and while there she found that the house was filled with mothers and babies. I climbed two flights of narrow, dirty stairs and saw Mrs. Gray, who said she would take the baby on full surrender only, for $50. She said the mother could never know what became of the child afterwards.

AFRAID OF DISCOVERY

"I get lots of children; but one has to be careful, as there are so many schemes going around. I had a woman come here the other day that acted as if she were a detective. I gave her no information. One never knows when they will get caught up."

Mrs. Gray then brought an infant from an inner room and showed it to us. As I grew liberal with my price she grew more confidential, but throughout the interview she displayed a shrewdness and a fear of betraying something.

"I had a woman come to me one day and say that her husband threatened to leave her if she did not party with a child she had previous to the marriage. She got me to take the child and put it in a home. She paid me well and paid the child's board, visiting it every week, while the husband thought she did not know where it was. It is now seven years old. Burial permits are easy to get. I retain a reputable physician and he never asks any questions. Where do all the babies go? Why, rich people adopt them, of course." I promised her the baby and a fifty-dollar bill, and I was never to know anything of it afterwards.

DR. MAY—W. 24th, graduate of university, Phil., Pa; 25 years' experience, skillful, safe treatment; one interview sufficient, consultation strictly private.

I called on Dr. May and I really thought the man was insane. In order to inspire us with confidence he told of the most criminal actions. He readily consented to take charge of the child for the modest sum of $500, and he told us he could not be asked to do anything that he would refuse. He showed us diplomas from a New York and also a Philadelphia medical college. He also said he belonged to the Board of Health and was a member in good standing in the Masonic lodge. Notwithstanding all this, he confessed to the most criminal actions, and when we started to go he asked me if I had any money with me. I said no, and then he begged that I give him, if but 25 cents, to retain his services, I shudder when I think of what a horrible creature he is, according to his own confession, yet see the position that at least he claims to hold.

"A physician is bound not to reveal the secrets of his patients," he said. "Once I was taken to court in a divorce case. It was just another story of a jealous husband and pretty wife in love with her physician, but I refused to reveal anything, and the man lost his case. An insurance company also took me upon a case where a man died of hard drink. I treated him for it; but I would not tell, and so the company was the loser. Women always trust me. They know that once they pay me I'm bound not to tell on them."

CHILDREN ADOPTED FOR A PURPOSE

LADIES can confidently consult Mrs. K. Gollas, ladies' physician, West 29th st.

Mrs. Golias was at home and ready to be consulted. She would take the child for $35. "I always have children taken away by the time they are a day old. It is a great deal of trouble to have several months-old babies adopted. Why? Well, women want to pass the babies for their own and so they get them young. I have had women come from France and Germany to adopt a child. They have had property that depended on an heir, or they wanted to cheat other relatives out of it, and so buy a child. Customers always say what complexion they want the babe. I think they are all rich people who take the children, for what would poor people want with them? We never know anything about the child afterwards. The charitable homes where infants are taken, are horrible places. Last summer at one asylum the babies died by the hundreds. I keep a physician who gives burial permits for infants or adults who die in my house. The mothers seldom, if ever, keep their children. A short time ago a woman gave up her babe, and the parties who adopted it told me accidentally that they had bought a home on Long Island and from whom I told the woman, and strange as it may seem, they had bought their home from her father who is a farmer, and would be her neighbor, though they never knew it. So you see the woman can see her child every day."

I visited the New York Foundling Asylum in Sixty-eighth street, near Third avenue. The Sister at the desk kept attending to her finger nails while I was talking to her. "I will only make arrangements with the mother. If she gives us the child, she never sees or hears from it again. We only take full surrender and no one can know where they go."

As I left the asylum I met sixty-two girls in blue dresses and 100 boys in line, crossing Lexington Avenue. I do not know where they were from, but their orphanage was stamped on them.

NELLIE BLY BUYS A BABY
NELLIE BLY

THE NEW YORK WORLD
OCTOBER 6, 1889

AN INNOCENT CHILD SOLD INTO SLAVERY FOR TEN DOLLARS.

THE APPALLING TRAFFIC IN HUMAN FLESH IN NEW YORK

HEARTLESS MOTHERS AND GRASPING MIDWIVES WHO BARTER HELPLESS CHILDREN FOR MONEY—SHOCKING INDIFFERENCE OF THE SLAVE-DEALERS AS TO WHAT BECOMES OF THE LITTLE ONES—NO QUESTIONS ASKED—A VISIT TO THE MIDWIFE WHO SOLD THE BOGUS HAMILTON BABY—STARTLING FACTS WHICH WILL APPEAL TO EVERY LOVING MOTHER IN THE LAND.

I bought a baby last week, to learn how baby slaves are bought and sold in the city of New York. Think of it! An immortal soul bartered for $10. Fathers—mothers—ministers—missionaries, I bought an immortal soul last week for $10!

We had a war not many years ago—a long and bitter struggle, which cost many millions of lives and many millions of dollars, and it was supposed that slavery had ended when the armies disbanded.

But it did not stop slavery. Slavery exists today in New York in a more repulsive form than it ever existed in the South. White slaves, baby slaves—young, innocent, helpless baby slaves—bought and sold every day in the week—bargained for before they are born—sold by their parents! The negro slaves had a John Brown to start their march to freedom. Who will start it for the baby slaves of New York?

For several days before I bought a baby I advertised in a number of newspapers for a baby to adopt. I received no reply. Why? Because people who adopt babies for good purposes and in a legitimate way do not expect to buy them. Those people who have babies in the market expect to sell them, and they will not give them away.

THE BABY

I went first to see Mrs. Dr. Dimire, as her sign reads. She lives in a comfortable house in West Forty-eighth street. A neatly dressed maid ushered me into a very homelike and artistic parlor. The floor was softly carpeted, the windows were hung with real lace curtains, and there was some valuable bric-a-brac about and handsome jardinières and pictures. Large, rolling glass doors shut off a small room in the rear. When the door opened to admit Mme. Dimire two Skye terriers troubled over each other in their rush to get in first. Mme. Dimire is a large, fleshy woman, with a double chin and dark eyes. She wore a loose wrapper of some thin material that was as white as the spotless cat which lay snuggled up in the window.

"Are you Dr. Dimire?" I asked.

"Yes," she replied, motioning me to be seated.

"Did you advertise a baby for sale?"

"Yes," she replied again, smiling still broader. "Do you want a baby?"

"Yes. Have you the baby still?"

"Well, you are the eighth person that has called for that baby today," she replied complacently, folding her arms across her ampleness. "It has gone now to the doctor's with a lady who wanted a baby. She wanted a boy, though, and a fair one. She said her doctor could tell how babies will turn out, so she has taken the nurse and the baby to the doctor to see if it will be fair. I am expecting her every moment now with an answer, but there is another woman upstairs who is very anxious for it. She wanted a boy, but this girl baby is so beautiful that she will take it if the other woman does not. How old do you want the baby to be?"

"Quite young," I said slowly, for I had not thought much about age. I expected, however, they would at least be several weeks old.

"Well, this baby was born at 7 o'clock Saturday morning. That is old enough if you are going to pass it off as your own. Are you married?" she asked suddenly.

"Is it necessary for me to tell about myself in order to buy a baby? I thought not," I answered evasively.

NOT INQUISITIVE

"I don't want to know anything about you. I never remember ladies I have business with" she said, with a laugh. "When I am paid and a child is taken out of here that is as far as I am concerned. You look so young that I could not believe you wanted the baby for yourself."

"I supposed you never asked where the baby was going or what use was to be made of it?" I said stiffly.

"I don't," she answered quickly. "I never tell who its parents are; I never know who takes it. The moment it is born I send it to my nurse, who does not live here. There it remains until somebody takes it. The children born here are all of aristocratic parentage. I never take common people in. Just now I sent a woman to my nurse's for care, because she did not belong to the class that patronizes me. What did you expect to pay for a baby?"

"I did not know, as I never bought one." I replied hesitatingly, "How much do you charge for one?"

"I don't sell babies," she replied, "but people are expected to pay me something. How much are you willing to give?"

"Ten dollars!" I said, remembering the price paid for the Robert Ray Hamilton baby.

"Oh, my no!" she said scornfully. "I never get less than $25. The woman who has the baby this afternoon said she would give me $50 if she took it. If she does not take it will you give $25? Hurry, for there is a woman waiting now who is anxious to take it."

"If it suits me I will give you $25 for it," I replied.

Mme. Dimire then said that she would see the woman who was waiting for the baby and, if possible, persuade her to buy the one that was expected to arrive at the house inside of forty-eight hours. If the woman consented she would then give me the address of her nurse and I could go to see the baby. The woman concluded with the proviso that if I did not like the baby I would come back to Mme. Dimire's, where she would wait for my report.

SUSPICIOUS OF DANGER

"Now, before I give you this," said the madame, indicating a note which was to be my key to the baby slave's presence. "I want you to give me your word of honor that you are not a lady detective."

"Why!" I exclaimed, with an injured air, "What a dreadful idea! How can you imagine such a thing for a moment?"

"I must protect myself," she said apologetically. "If you had come alone and then published what I have said, I could swear that you lied; but as you have a witness," indicating my elderly companion, "I could not do it; so I want your word before I trust you with my nurse's address."

"I don't see how you can imagine such a thing," I said sadly. "I am just as anxious as you are for secrecy."

"You evade my question," she said suspiciously.

"I am not a detective," I said positively. This satisfied the woman, and she gave me the sheet of paper on which was written the nurse's name and address, with this below it:

"Please show the little girl and tell what that lady has decided."

In a tenement-house in East Fifty-second street I found the nurse. She lives in three rooms on the second floor.

"Don't ask for her in the halls or let anyone know what you go to see her about," cautioned Mme. Dimire.

Still, I did ask one woman I met in the hallway. When I was leaving she came into the same flat, so I suppose she was a member of the nurse's family. The flat was small and dirty. I asked for the nurse by name. A woman, with ample shape, greasy dress and a great space between the eyes, who met me at the door, claimed the name as hers. She was very gruff and suspicious, and when I told her I had come to see the baby she never moved a muscle and wanted to know what baby. Then I gave her the note madame had given me.

OUT IN THE RAIN

"I just got in with the baby," she said, snappishly, "I've had it out most all day with a common sort of a woman who made believe she wanted her doctor to tell if it would be fair or dark. It caught a cold, I guess, and I have just done givin' it some oil."

She took us into the tiny front room of the flat, but before we sat down she invited us to return to the kitchen. Two small, dirty girls, who in nowise resembled each other, followed her about.

"I guess you can see her here better than in the front room," she said.

In one dark corner was a small cook stove. Near it was a window. Almost touching the stove was a rocking-chair. On a pillow in that chair and covered with a shawl was the baby slave. The nurse pulled down the shawl and I leaned over to look at the tiny mite, the little slave, who was but two days' old, and had been handled and examined by many with a view to buying it. My heart ached for that poor slave. A two-days'-old baby out on a rainy day for many hours!

But it stretches itself. Its little face is awfully red and it has such dark hair and such heavy eyebrows and such a straight nose, which the nurse tells me is a wonderful thing for a two days'-old babe. But its tiny hands are whiter than the pillow it rests on. It works its little fingers feebly, almost as if it wanted to put them in its little mouth. It moves again and strange cries comes from its tiny throat.

"She caught a cold to-day," the nurse explained in answer to my startled question. "She cried all the afternoon. I made a long trip and I guess she was cold. That's what makes her hoarse now. I gave her a big dose of oil and I think she will be all right tomorrow. Do you want me to undress her?"

OPEN TO INSPECTION

"Oh, no: please don't. What would you do that for?" I said, all in a breath.

"Most everybody that buys a baby makes me undress it a dozen times before they're sure it's all right. This is a lovely girl though, big for its age," she said as she lifted it out of the chair. The poor little slave twisted up its tiny face, then it opened its tiny dark eyes and blinked just as if it wanted to ask me to buy it. I could not stand it. I turned my back and asked her to put it down.

Hurrying from the house. I returned to Mme. Dimire's. I left my companion in the coupe this time, for I only intended to make my report.

"Madame, the woman took the baby to her doctor's and then sent the nurse home, saying she would come over to see you. The baby has a dreadful cold and even if the woman does not take it I would be afraid to after it was so exposed. I am dreadful afraid of death and I don't want to buy a baby that is going to die."

"That woman has treated me badly," she replied sternly. "This is the second time I have fussed with her. If she doesn't take this she will have to go somewhere else the next time."

"I would rather wait and take my chances on the next you have for sale." I said pleasantly.

"I cannot keep a baby for you unless you give me a deposit," she said cunningly. "The reason I asked you so many questions" going back to our former interview, "was because you looked too young to be married and wanting a baby. You had a lady with you who looked very smart. She wouldn't say a word, so she could say she wasn't guilty. If anything happened. I am not responsible if a woman gets a baby from me and then pretends to her husband it is her own. I nearly got in trouble, and may yet, by giving a baby to a woman who came here accompanied by another woman just as you did to-day. I was the one who furnished the Hamilton baby."

"Robert Ray Hamilton's baby!" I exclaimed in surprise.

SHE SOLD THE HAMILTON BABY

"Yes, the very same. Mrs. Hamilton came here with Mrs. Swinton for a baby. Mrs. Hamilton looked as if she was in good circumstances; she was dressed expensively and Mrs. Swinton looked respectable enough, though awfully cunning. I didn't like to give a baby, when there was a witness, just as I felt to-day in your case, so I said to Mrs. Hamilton, 'Does your husband know that you are going to adopt a baby?' She laughed and said, 'Oh, yes, he known I am going to get on,' and Mrs. Swinton said, 'You don't need to be afraid to give us the baby, for my son is her husband!'

Mme. Dimire asked a flood of questions about my domestic affairs. She wanted to give me advice about the way to deceive husbands, as she said she understood things much better than I could; she had had so much more experience. My replies showed my ignorance in many respects, and though she laughed at it, she was completely disarmed by my feigned frankness.

I afterwards visited a number of places, always with the same result. There were babies to be had for the money. Still, I must make two exceptions. Dr. O'Reilly, of West Forty-ninth street, was very sharp. He is a tall man, with smooth face, stubby gray hair and a stutter. He occupies an entire house, as does Mme. Dimire, and, like hers, it is always filled with high-priced patients. "This is the hi-hi-hi-highest priced place in New York," he said proudly, as he looked at me with an impudent, suspicious look. "I cha-cha-charge $100 entrance fee, and everything else accordingly. This is the only place, the only place where aristocratic children can be found. W-w-when I take a patient in her offspring is signed over to me to do as I like with it."

"You ask no questions of those who take the babies?" I asked.

"N-n-never," he answered giving me an evil look. "I don't want to know who or what they are or what becomes of the baby. Th-th-that's nothing to me."

The other exception was a woman on the east side who said she had no babies, and never had. She claims that she always makes the mother take her child away with her and does her utmost to persuade all the women not to part with their children. Her house, she says, is always open to any officers of the law who may wish to inspect it. As she carries on a legitimate business she has nothing to conceal, so she says.

Mrs. Schroeder lives in East Fifty-eighth street. She runs a large establishment and always has babies for sale. She is very cunning. Nobody has ever learned who her nurse is. As soon as a baby is born in her house it is wrapped in a blanket and taken to the nurse's. Then she advertises "babies adopted," which means she both buys and sells. She buys the baby from the mother, according to an agreement made on entering her house, for some sum not exceeding one dollar! She sells for what she can get.

PRICE-LIST OF BABIES

"I have no baby here now," she said to me. This is her regular plea. "If you set an hour for coming back I will get a baby for you. How much? Oh, now, I don't dare sell babies; but, of course, you will expect to pay me for my trouble. Say $15. No? Well, then, $10. You can't expect much of a baby, nor one of good, respectable parents, for $10!"

I did not return. If she would not send me to her nurse's I had no interest in returning. There had been a baby born in her house the day I was there.

Mrs. White, in East Forty-ninth street, buys and sells babies. She has a fine private house, and claims acquaintance with a number of society men and women. She sells a baby for what she can get, but she expects to get a good price.

"I have babies every day," she told me. "A lady from Brooklyn secured one here this morning. If you wait an hour or so I will have one for you."

"A boy or girl?" I asked sarcastically.

"Oh, now, you wouldn't expect me to tell that," she laughed. "If you don't want to wait give me a deposit and I will keep it for you."

"It is quite too new for me. I want to see the baby before I buy it." I said, and I went elsewhere.

"You can never get a baby from more desirable people than this will be." She said, at the door. "The girl belongs to wealthy people. Her mother brought her here, and when she recovers she will go back home and someday marry. Her father doesn't know anything about it. He thinks she is visiting friends. It's an easy thing to do, and is done every day in New York."

Mrs. Eppinger lives in East Eighteenth street. She is a short woman with a shrewd face, and wears a nurse's cap and apron. Mrs. Eppinger furnished two of the Hamilton babies, both of which died.

A FINE GRADE OF BABIES

"You can get babies of good parents from Mrs. Dimire and myself, but no place else," she said, boastingly.

"How much do you charge for babies?" I asked boldly.

"I don't sell them, but I always get something for my trouble. The lady who bought the baby I have at my nurse's now gave me $20 for it. She put the money in my hands. I thought it was a silver dollar, but it was a twenty-dollar gold piece."

"DON'T YOU KEEP THE BABIES HERE?"

"Indeed I don't. The moment they are born I send for my nurse and she takes them away and keeps them until they are taken by somebody."

"You never ask any questions of the persons who buy the babies?" I asked.

"Indeed I don't. I don't want to know anything about them."

Sold to the highest bidder, let them be what they may, let them buy for any purpose they please! Sold by their parents and by the female slave-masters!

Every physician is required, so I believe, to make a report of every birth, with the names and ages of the parents, to the Board of Health. These dealers in baby slaves acknowledge averaging a birth a day, yet they make no report. This enormous birth-rate in these houses alone must make considerable difference in a year in the census of New York.

I bought my baby from Mrs. Koehler, of East Eighty-fourth street. She is about four feet high and three feet wide. She has been in trouble several times, but by some means she always manages to escape punishment. If she stole a loaf of bread she would be imprisoned, but as she only deals in human flesh she goes free.

"Mrs. Koehler, have you a baby to sell?" I asked, as I sat down in her well-furnished parlor.

"Yes, I have—one born at 2 o'clock this morning," She answered quickly. It was then 3 in the afternoon. "It is a girl. I will bring it to you," and the slave-dealer went out the door to get the baby slave.

I think probably there was a death in the house that day; at least a vase of tuberoses on the centre table suggested such an idea to me. Their perfume was very heavy and oppressive, and I moved nearer the darkened windows in a vain effort to gain a breath of fresh air.

ONLY HALF A DAY OLD

"Here is the girl," she said, re-entering the room with a bundle in her arms. She took it to a dark corner of the room for me to examine. Her excuse was that the light would hurt its eyes. In reality she wanted to prevent my seeing any blemishes there might be about the baby slave.

It was thirteen hours old, and I bought it. I had no nurse as yet, so I told Mrs. Koehler I would call for it the next day. The woman had been in difficulties before, as I have said, and she fixes up a dummy—a woman to represent the mother—whom she introduces to the buyers, so she may give her consent. Mrs. Koehler also gives what she pretends is an agreement. This also is to prevent the law from getting its clutches upon her; but it is perfectly worthless, so far as legality is concerned.

"How much do you want for the baby?" I asked when I returned the next day.

"Well, now, I can't set a price, I do not sell babies," she said.

She brought the baby into the room. She had been feeding it and the milk seemed to have such a peculiar tinge that it suggested ideas of drugs and such things. It is well known that babies are often drugged and live but a few days after leaving these slave-dealers' hands. Mrs. Eppinger sold Mrs. Hamilton two babies. They both died. Mrs. Koehler sold Mrs. Hamilton one baby. It died. None of these slave-dealers, with the exception of the one who did the business, knew what woman sold baby Beatrice who lived.

"Will you give your word that the baby is healthy and

perfect in every respect?" I asked the slave-dealer.

"Yes, it is a beautiful baby. Now, if you will pay me, we will go up to see the mother. She has never seen the baby yet."

I gave her $10. She looked at the money, then, holding the baby in one hand, she held out the other, saying:

"Please give me more. That is a very little price for such a baby. Won't you pay me more?"

"Not another cent now," I replied. "If the baby turns out well I will send you a present."

I send her a copy of the SUNDAY WORLD containing this article, with my compliments.

A DUMMY-MOTHER

On the third story, in a front room, lay a fair young woman. She had been talking to a friend who was visiting her.

"Here is the baby," the slave-dealer said.

"This is the young lady who wants it."

I knew the dummy-mother trick, so I asked the pretended mother what hour the baby was born. She turned to the slave-dealer for answer. She was handed the baby. She undid the shawl. The little slave, which I had just paid for, opened its tiny blue eyes, as if striving to see for the first and last time—its mother. It rolled its little head feebly: it worked its tiny hands. I felt my throat fill and Hood's cry enter my heart, "O God! that human flesh should be so cheap!"

"It's little, isn't it?" the woman remarked indifferently as she handed the slave back to the dealer, without one kiss, without one glance, without one prayer. If she was its mother her own baby was going from her forever. Where? She did not know. With whom? She did not ask. For what purpose? She did not care.

I took the badly written paper Mrs. Koehler handed me. This is what it said:

"In consideration of the sum of one dollar the party of the second part surrenders to the party of the first part her child, and it is agreed that the party of the first part may dispose of the said child in any manner."

The mother sold it for $1. I bought it for $10 from the

slave-dealer. This on the 2d of October, in the year of our Lord 1889.

The inhuman, barbarous transaction made me heartsick. I wanted to get away from the slave-dealer and her patients. Tenderly my companion wrapped the blue-eyed, day-old babe in a soft, warm shawl and we left the house as the slave-dealer called after me:

"Don't forget to send me more money for that baby. It's worth it."

ABOUT NELLIE BLY

Nellie Bly was born Elizabeth Cochran. Her father, a man of considerable wealth, served for many years as judge of Armstrong County, Pennsylvania. He lived on a large estate called Cochran's Mills, which took its name from him. There Elizabeth "Pink" Cochrane was born.

Being in reduced circumstances after her father's death, her mother remarried, only to divorce Jack Ford a few years later. The family then moved to Pittsburg, where a twenty-year-old Pink read a column in the *Pittsburg Dispatch* entitled "What Girls Are Good For." Enraged at the sexist and classist tone, she wrote a furious letter to the editor. Impressed, the editor engaged her to do special work for the newspaper as a reporter, writing under the name "Nellie Bly." Her first series of stories, "Our Workshop Girls," brought life and sympathy to working women in Pittsburgh.

A year later she went as a correspondent to Mexico, where she remained six months, sending back weekly articles. After her return she longed for broader fields, and so moved to New York. The story of her attempt to make a place for herself, or to find an opening, was a long one of disappointment, until at last she gained the attention of the *New York World*.

Her first achievement for them was the exposure of the Blackwell's Island Insane Asylum, in which she spent ten days, and two days in the Bellevue Insane Asylum. The story created a great sensation, making "Nellie Bly" a household name.

After three years of doing work as a "stunt girl" at the *World*, Bly conceived the idea of making a trip around the world in less time than had been done by Phileas Fogg, the fictitious hero of Jules Verne's famous novel. In fact, she made it in 72 days. On her return in January 1890 she was greeted by ovations all the way from San Francisco to New York.

She then paused her reporting career to write novels, but returned to the World three years later. In 1895 she married millionaire industrialist Robert Seaman, and a couple years later retired from journalism to take an interest in his factories.

She returned to journalism almost twenty years later, reporting on World War I from behind the Austrian lines. Upon returning to New York, she spent the last years of her life doing both reporting and charity work, finding homes for orphans. She died in 1922.

ABOUT THE AUTHOR

David Blixt is an author and actor living in Chicago. An Artistic Associate of the Michigan Shakespeare Festival, where he serves as the resident Fight Director, he is also co-founder of A Crew Of Patches Theatre Company, a Shakespearean repertory based in Chicago. He has acted and done fight work for the Goodman Theatre, Chicago Shakespeare Theatre, Steppenwolf, the Shakespeare Theatre of Washington DC, and First Folio Shakespeare, among many others.

As a writer, his STAR-CROSS'D series of novels place the characters of Shakespeare's Italian plays in their historical setting, drawing in figures such as Dante, Giotto, and Petrarch to create an epic of warfare, ingrigue, and romance. In HER MAJESTY'S WILL, Shakespeare himself becomes a character as Blixt explores Shakespeare's "Lost Years," teaming the young Will with the dark and devious Kit Marlowe to hilarious effect. In the COLOSSUS series, Blixt brings first century Rome and Judea to life as he relates the fall of Jerusalem, the building of the Colosseum, and the coming of Christianity to Rome. And in his bestselling NELLIE BLY series, he explores the amazing life and adventures of America's premier undercover reporter.

In 2019 David discovered eleven unknown novels by Nellie Bly,

David continues to write, act, and travel. He has ridden camels around the pyramids at Giza, been thrown out of the Vatican Museum and been blessed by John-Paul II, scaled the Roman ramp at Masada, crashed a hot-air balloon, leapt from cliffs on small Greek islands, dined with Counts and criminals, climbed to the top of Mount Sinai, and sat in the Prince's chair in Verona's palace. But David is happiest at his desk, weaving tales of brilliant people in dire and dramatic straits. Living with his wife and two children, David describes himself as "actor, author, father, husband - in reverse order."

WWW.DAVIDBLIXT.COM

Books by Nellie Bly

Ten Days in a Mad-House
Six Months In Mexico
Nellie Bly's Book: Around the World in 72 Days

The Lost Novels of Nellie Bly

the Mystery of Central Park
Eva the Adventuress
New York by Night
Alta Lynn, M.D.
Wayne's Faithful Sweetheart
Little Luckie
Dolly the Coquette
in Love with a Stranger
the Love of Three Girls
Little Penny, Child of the Streets
Pretty Merribelle
Twins and Rivals

BOOKS BY DAVID BLIXT

NELLIE BLY
WHAT GIRLS ARE GOOD FOR
CHARITY GIRL
A VERY CLEVER GIRL

THE STAR-CROSS'D SERIES
THE MASTER OF VERONA
VOICE OF THE FALCONER
FORTUNE'S FOOL
THE PRINCE'S DOOM
VARNISH'D FACES: STAR-CROSS'D SHORT STORIES

WILL & KIT
HER MAJESTY'S WILL

THE COLOSSUS SERIES
COLOSSUS: STONE & STEEL
COLOSSUS: THE FOUR EMPERORS

NON-FICTION

ORIGIN OF THE FEUD BY DAVID BLIXT
TOMORROW & TOMORROW BY DAVID AND JANICE L BLIXT
FIGHTING WORDS: A COMBAT GLOSSARY EDITED BY DAVID BLIXT

PLAYSCRIPTS

ACTION MOVIE - THE PLAY BY JOE FOUST AND RICHARD RAGSDALE
ALL CHILDISH THINGS BY JOSEPH ZETTELMAIER
THE COUNT OF MONTE CRISTO ADAPTED BY CHRISTOPHER M WALSH
DEAD MAN'S SHOES BY JOSEPH ZETTELMAIER
THE DECADE DANCE BY JOSEPH ZETTELMAIER
EBENEZER: A CHRISTMAS PLAY BY JOSEPH ZETTELMAIER
EVE OF IDES - A PLAY BY DAVID BLIXT
THE GRAVEDIGGER: A FRANKENSTEIN PLAY BY JOSEPH ZETTELMAIER
HATFIELD & MCCOY BY SHAWN PFAUTSCH
HER MAJESTY'S WILL ADAPTED BY ROBERT KAUZLARIC
IT CAME FROM MARS BY JOSEPH ZETTELMAIER
THE MOONSTONE ADAPTED BY ROBERT KAUZLARIC
NORTHERN AGGRESSION BY JOSEPH ZETTELMAIER
ONCE A PONZI TIME BY JOE FOUST
THE RENAISSANCE MAN BY JOSEPH ZETTELMAIER
THE SCULLERY MAID BY JOSEPH ZETTELMAIER
SEASON ON THE LINE BY SHAWN PFAUTSCH
STAGE FRIGHT: A HORROR ANTHOLOGY BY JOSEPH ZETTELMAIER
A TALE OF TWO CITIES ADAPTED BY CHRISTOPHER M WALSH
WILLIAMSTON ANTHOLOGY: VOLUME 1
WILLIAMSTON ANTHOLOGY: VOLUME 2

WWW.SORDELETINK.COM

Manufactured by Amazon.ca
Bolton, ON

29860266R00072